The baby had to come first.

Both men started to move. She saw one of them grab the carrier seat with the baby, and the other took some keys from his pocket.

Holden got them moving, too. Fast. Off the porch, and he headed straight for the car. The moment they reached it, he maneuvered her to the far side away from the house, and they ducked down.

He pulled out a knife from his pocket and jammed it into the front tire and went to the rear to do the same. That would slow them down, but it wouldn't stop them. Those men were in a hurry to get out of there, and they'd drive on the rims if they had to.

The men raced out the door of the house, making a beeline for the car. They were just yards away when Nicky heard a sound she didn't want to hear.

Footsteps.

Behind Holden and her.

Holden pivoted, aiming his gun, but it was already too late.

HOLDEN

—

USA TODAY Bestselling Author

DELORES FOSSEN

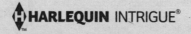
HARLEQUIN INTRIGUE®

Recycling programs
for this product may
not exist in your area.

ISBN-13: 978-0-373-75661-2

Holden

Printed in U.S.A.

Delores Fossen, a *USA TODAY* bestselling author, has sold over fifty novels with millions of copies of her books in print worldwide. She's received a Booksellers' Best Award and an RT Reviewers' Choice Best Book Award. She was also a finalist for a prestigious RITA® Award. Contact her at www.deloresfossen.com.

Books by Delores Fossen

Harlequin Intrigue

The Lawmen of Silver Creek Ranch

Grayson
Dade
Nate
Kade
Gage
Mason
Josh
Sawyer
Landon
Holden

Appaloosa Pass Ranch

Lone Wolf Lawman
Taking Aim at the Sheriff
Trouble with a Badge
The Marshal's Justice
Six-Gun Showdown
Laying Down the Law

HQN Books

The McCord Brothers

Texas on My Mind
Lone Star Nights
Blame It on the Cowboy

Visit the Author Profile page at Harlequin.com for more titles.

CAST OF CHARACTERS

Holden Ryland—A marshal who learns his late brother and sister-in-law's embryo was stolen and implanted into a surrogate for the sole purpose of demanding money from his family. Holden must find the child and bring the people responsible to justice. He'll do that even if he has to team up with his ex, a woman he's not sure he can trust.

Nicky Hart—An investigative reporter who's often clashed with Holden and his family, but her late sister was married to Holden's brother, so the missing baby is also her nephew. Holden is her best chance at finding the newborn, and that means putting their troubled past behind them.

Oscar Hart—Nicky's father. He's been involved in plenty of shady businesses and was so desperate for a grandchild and heir that he could be the one behind this black-market baby deal.

Senator Lee Minton—He and his wife visited the same fertility clinic that's connected to the black-market baby operation, and now the senator is missing.

Beatrice Minton—Lee's wife. She claims she has no idea who took her husband or who's behind the stolen embryo, but having Lee's child could give her access to his wealthy estate—especially if Lee is never found.

Amanda Monroe—She was once the office manager at the fertility clinic in question, and now she claims someone is trying to kill her.

Carter Ryland—The newborn at the center of the fertility-clinic scheme.

Chapter One

Something wasn't right.

US Marshal Holden Ryland didn't have to rely on his lawman's instincts to know that. The Craftsman-style house was pitch-dark except for a single dim light in the front room. The home owner, Nicky Hart, hated the dark, and whenever she was home, every light was usually blazing.

So, either she'd skipped out on their little chat, or... Holden decided to go with the skipping-out theory because at the moment it was the lesser of two evils. After all, there was a reason why they needed to talk.

A bad one.

Holden slid his hand over the gun in his holster and got out of his truck. He'd barely made it a few steps when her white cat came darting out from beneath the porch. It headed right toward him, coiling around his leg and meowing.

Another sign that something was wrong.

Nicky didn't let the cat outside—ever.

So, was Nicky inside? And if so, had something happened to her? Holden cursed himself for not having done a silent approach. That way, he could have parked up the street, slipped around to the side of the house and looked in the windows. It might have alerted her neighbors, but that was better than dealing with some of the bad scenarios going through his head. Still, he hadn't taken that precaution because he hadn't figured he would run in to any kind of immediate trouble.

Well, no trouble other than an argument with Nicky.

When he'd called Nicky an hour earlier and told her that he was on his way to their hometown of Silver Creek to talk to her, she hadn't said a word about anything being wrong. In fact, she sounded as if she'd been expecting his call. But then, she'd sent a text just a few minutes later, saying she wouldn't be available after all.

Right.

Holden wasn't about to believe that lie. She was dodging him. And not doing a very good job of it, either, because her garage door was up, and he could see her car. That meant she was probably inside and that there was a good explanation for no lights on and the cat being outside. He hoped there was a good explanation anyway.

He kept watch around him, kept watch of the house, too, and made his way to the porch. However, before Holden could even ring the bell, the front door flew open, and he braced himself for what he might see.

But it was only Nicky.

He looked at her, from head to toe. She was wearing jeans and an old concert T-shirt, and had her auburn hair pulled back in a sloppy ponytail. No visible injuries or signs of distress. She was scowling at him, but over the past year or so, that was the norm whenever she laid eyes on him.

"Didn't you get my text?" she asked.

"Got it. Ignored it. Because we need to talk." Holden moved to go around her and inside, but she stepped in front of him, blocking his path.

"It's not a good time." She paused. "I'm expecting someone."

All right. That gave him a new theory. Maybe Nicky had a hot date who was on the way over. That might explain the lack of lights if she was aiming for something romantic.

A thought that bothered him a lot more than it should have.

Nicky was an attractive woman. Bullheaded and reckless, too. And she was married to her job as an investigative reporter. That said, she was still human and she probably did have a man in her life.

It still didn't mean Holden was going to skip that talk with her. He wouldn't.

Because he needed her to know that she was on the verge of being arrested.

He owed her that much. Barely. After the stunt she'd pulled last year, though, some members of his family might believe he owed her nothing. Still, here he was. He didn't play Mr. Nice Guy very often, and he hoped he didn't regret it this time.

"Tomorrow, you'll get a visit from an FBI agent," he told her.

Nicky didn't even blink. "I don't have time for this." And she would have shut the door in his face, if Holden hadn't blocked it with his foot. The edge of the door smacked against his cowboy boot.

"Make time," he snarled.

She blew out a quick breath. "Look, I know you're still in love with me," she said, "but you have to leave."

Holden tightened the grip on his gun. Yeah, something was definitely wrong. Because there was no way in hell he was in love with Nicky, and she knew it, too.

She shook her head, just a little, and glanced

at the hold that he had on his gun. Was she telling him not to draw? Or was that head shake about something else?

Holden intended to find out.

But it was best not to confront this head-on. Because the living room behind her was dark, he couldn't tell if there was someone waiting in the shadows. Someone armed and ready to kill her. Or maybe she'd discovered her house was bugged and she didn't want to say anything incriminating.

Holden hoped it was the second option.

"I'll be back tomorrow," Holden lied. "And we *will* talk then."

Leaving was a risk—anything he did at this point could be. But Holden hoped if there was someone inside that it was a good sign that the person had let Nicky answer the door. The person didn't want her dead.

Not yet anyway.

In her quest to get info on a story she was working on, she could have gotten herself mixed up with some very dangerous people, and that involvement might be coming back to bite her. To bite him, too, since Holden had to see what was going on. This was well past being a nice guy.

This had just become the job.

He drove his truck up a block, parked and

fired off a quick text to his cousin Landon, who was now a deputy in Silver Creek. Holden didn't request backup but told Landon that if he didn't hear from him in fifteen minutes, to send some help—fast.

With that done, Holden hurried to Nicky's house. Not going through the front yard but rather through the back. The houses in the small neighborhood didn't have fences, but there were plenty of mature trees that he ducked behind and used for cover. The darkness helped, too, and for once he was glad Nicky didn't have all the lights blazing.

Holden knew the layout of her house. He'd even spent the night there a couple of times, and he knew the best way to approach this wasn't through the back porch. Instead, he drew his gun and went to the French doors off her bedroom.

Unlocked.

He silently cursed. Since Nicky was afraid of the dark, you'd think she would be equally concerned with locking up, but Holden knew she could be lax about that.

He eased open the door, slipped into her bedroom and stood there. Listening. He didn't hear anything at first, only someone moving around in the living room where he'd last seen Nicky.

"You'd better be sure he doesn't come back,"

someone said. A man. And Holden didn't recognize his voice.

In case this was a lover she was meeting, Holden waited for more. He didn't have to wait very long.

"If that marshal does come back, I'll kill him," the man growled.

Hell. So, probably not a lover unless it was some jealous nut-job. Holden sent a second text to Landon requesting that backup, and he made his way to the bedroom door and then into the hall.

The house was old and had creaky floors in spots. He prayed he didn't step on one of those because he wanted to get the drop on whoever it was that had just threatened to kill him.

"The marshal won't be back," Nicky assured the man. "Not until tomorrow anyway."

"He said the FBI was coming. Your doing?" her visitor demanded.

"Hardly. The FBI will be looking for the same thing you want. Something I don't have."

Holden didn't know specifically what she was talking about, but it might have something to do with her latest project. A state senator who'd been missing over two weeks. Nicky had been investigating his disappearance and had cut some corners. Ones that could land her in jail.

Of course, at the moment that seemed to be the least of her worries.

"You have those files all right," the man argued. "Now, where are they? And don't try to hold any of them back. I want every file you stole from Conceptions Clinic."

Everything inside Holden went still.

Conceptions Clinic?

It was the name of the fertility clinic that Holden knew well, and just hearing it brought back some painful memories. Of his brother Emmett and his brother's wife, Annie. Annie had been Nicky's sister, and now both Emmett and Annie were dead. Annie had died in a car accident, but that hadn't been the cause of Emmett's death.

No. He'd been murdered only months after Annie's death. His killer was dead, but that didn't soften the blow for Holden. Emmett wasn't coming back from the grave just because the Rylands had managed to get justice for him.

Before their deaths, Emmett and Annie made multiple trips to Conceptions Fertility Clinic in San Antonio with the hopes of finally getting the baby they so desperately wanted. But that hadn't happened. Because they'd both died before the process could be completed.

So, why would Nicky steal files from the place now?

"You're either going to give those files to me now, or I'll start putting bullets in you," the man warned her. "I won't kill you, yet, but I'll make you wish you were dead."

Every word of that threat put Holden on higher and higher alert, and he had to move fast.

Still trying to keep quiet, Holden hurried to the end of the hall and peered into the living room. Nicky was still by the front door, and there was a man between Holden and her. And yeah, the guy had a gun pointed right at her.

Nicky didn't say a word, but her eyes widened just a fraction when she saw Holden, and the man must have noticed even her slight reaction. He pivoted, taking aim at Holden.

The thug fired.

Not a loud blast. He was using a silencer on his gun.

Holden jumped out of the way just in time, and the bullet tore through a chunk of the wall.

"Get down," Holden shouted to Nicky, but she was already doing just that.

She scrambled behind the sofa. It wouldn't give her much cover, but Holden was counting on this moron shooting at him instead of her.

And that's just what he did.

The gunman ducked down beside a chair and fired another shot at Holden. Then, another. The shots wouldn't be loud enough to get the attention of the neighbors, which was a good thing. Holden didn't want bystanders hurrying over to Nicky's house to check on this.

Whatever *this* was.

"You want him to die?" the man barked. "Because that's what'll happen if you don't tell him to get the hell out of here."

Holden wasn't going anywhere. He dropped lower to the ground, leaned out and fired a shot at the guy. However, before Holden could even tell if he'd hit him, all hell broke loose.

There was the sound of something metal clanking onto the floor, and a few seconds later, tear gas began to spew through the room. The effects were instant. Holden's gray eyes burned like fire, and he started to cough. He could hear Nicky having a coughing fit, too.

But not the man.

Maybe he'd brought a gas mask or something because Holden heard him take off running, and saw him bolt out the back door.

Even though he was coughing too hard to catch his breath, Holden hurried after the guy, but he'd only made it a few steps when Nicky called out to him.

"Let him go. We have to leave now." Covering her mouth with her hand, she staggered her way to him, caught him by the wrist and led him toward the side entrance to the garage.

"Landon will be here soon," he choked out.

"We don't have time to wait around for him. Please, we need to go."

Holden didn't fight her as they'd gone into the garage because he welcomed the fresh air. Also welcomed getting into her car since he didn't want to be standing out in the open with that gunman still out there. But he did clamp his hand over hers when she tried to drive away.

"What the hell's going on?" he demanded. "Who was that man and what files did you steal?"

Nicky shook her head, fighting to get his grip off her, but Holden held on.

"The people at Conceptions Clinic did some very bad things. There are babies in danger," Nicky said, her breath shivering. "And one of them is *our* nephew."

Chapter Two

Nicky knew that Holden had plenty of questions, but she couldn't wait any longer. That gunman who'd broken into her house was no doubt on the way to the person who hired him.

And that person might move the baby before she could get to him.

"We have to get out of here fast," she reminded him.

Even though Nicky was still coughing, she threw the car into Reverse and gunned the engine despite the fact that Holden still had his hand gripped around hers.

Nicky didn't look at him. Partly because she was trying to maneuver her car out of the garage. Hard to do that, though, with him holding on. He finally let go.

"Start talking," Holden insisted. He, too, was still coughing and rubbing his eyes. "I want answers, and I want them now."

Easier said than done. There were a lot of pieces to this puzzle, some that could get her arrested, but the only one that mattered right now was the baby. Nicky had failed her sister in so many ways, but she couldn't fail this time.

"Who was that man?" Holden added when she didn't say anything.

"A hired thug. I don't know his name, but I'm sure he's already told his boss what happened."

And what had happened was that things had just fallen apart. Nicky had thought she had more time, hours at least, to come up with a plan. But time had just run out.

She couldn't help herself. The tears came, and she tried to fight them back. The tears wouldn't save Annie's baby. Right now, she had to focus and get to the hotel as soon as possible.

"Where are we going?" Holden demanded, and he took out his phone and texted someone.

Probably one of his cousins or brothers. They were all lawmen, and under different circumstances, they might be able to help. But in this case, they could make things much, much worse.

"The Victorian bed-and-breakfast about ten miles from here."

"The place out in the middle of nowhere?" he asked.

She nodded. "I'm pretty sure that's where they're holding the baby."

Holden cursed and sent another text. "There'd better be a damn good explanation as to why you're *pretty sure* about that. And there'd also better be an equally good explanation as to why you told me Emmett and Annie had a baby."

It was hard to think with everything racing through her mind, with her heart racing, too, but she tried. Sometime in the next five minutes she needed to convince Holden that he had to help her.

"This all started when I was investigating the missing senator, Lee Minton," she said. "I found out he and his wife had gone to Conceptions Fertility Clinic around the same time as Emmett and Annie. So, I went to Conceptions, too, not expecting to find much, but they stonewalled me. That made me push even harder to find out what they were hiding."

He mumbled, "Right." Probably a dig at the fact that she usually pushed too hard. Sometimes, with deadly consequences.

"And what they were hiding was a baby? Emmett and Annie's baby?" There was a boatload of skepticism in his voice.

Once, she'd been plenty skeptical, too. If she hadn't been, if she'd jumped on this earlier, they might not be racing to save a child.

"Yes, their baby," Nicky affirmed. "And don't ask why they did all of this because I don't know. Not yet anyway. But I think it might somehow be connected to the senator's disappearance." But she could be a long way from figuring how exactly.

"Senator Minton?" he asked, though he probably wasn't asking for clarification but was rather puzzled as to how Minton would play into this. The answer was maybe he didn't, but the senator had been missing for two weeks now, and it was while looking for him that she'd stumbled on to Conceptions.

"Yes, Senator Lee Minton," she confirmed.

"How are you sure of any of this?" Holden snapped.

Oh, he was not going to like this. "I hacked into the clinic's computer and copied some files," she added. "Hacked into the senator's computer, too, and then I put a listening device in Conceptions Clinic."

Now, Holden's cursing got a whole lot worse. For good reason. Because she'd just rattled off enough crimes to put her in jail. But she'd had an even better reason to do this.

To save Annie's son.

"That's what the thug was talking about," Holden snarled. "Where are the files and what's in them?"

Nicky decided to skip the *where* part and

move to the *what*. Just in case the thug had managed to turn the tables on her and bug her car.

"The ones I copied from Conceptions were marked 'the Genesis Project,'" she explained. "No names were connected with them, just case numbers, and when I looked at one, I figured out from the dates that the case number was Annie and Emmett's."

She'd tell him about the other info in them later. For now, Nicky focused on taking the road to the B and B.

"I don't know who did it, but someone stole Annie and Emmett's embryo and implanted it into a surrogate. And last week, the surrogate gave birth to a boy." Nicky turned off her car's headlights as she approached the B and B, and she pulled off the road, parking behind some trees.

Holden shook his head, stayed quiet a moment. "Could be it was a mix-up. Or maybe the embryo was donated to another couple who used a surrogate?"

Mercy, she wanted to latch onto that and believe it. "Then, why did that man just threaten me?"

"I don't know. Maybe you stole more than one set of files or pissed off more than just these people. Or it could have something to do with why the FBI wants to arrest you."

Even if it was true, it was still too big of a risk to let them move the baby. Of course, Holden might not believe there was a baby. He soon would, though.

"Who's inside that place?" he asked.

"Probably more men like the one who came to my house tonight." Hired guns to protect very precious cargo until they could get her father to pay up. "Look, I don't have time to explain all of this, but if they move the baby, we might never find him."

She didn't voice her greatest fear, that the goons inside might try to harm him so there'd be no proof of what they'd done.

"What if there really is a baby inside?" he went on. "How would we even know if it's Emmett and Annie's?"

She motioned toward her hair. "According to what I heard from the eavesdropping device, he's a ginger." *Not exactly rare but at least it was something like Annie and me.* Besides, she thought she might recognize her own sister's child.

"You have backup on the way?" she asked.

Holden nodded. "It's Landon. I told him to do a silent approach." He tipped his head to the house. "If the guy who was at your house had already contacted them, they could shoot us on sight."

"No. They want me alive so I can tell them where the files are. That's why he didn't kill me right away when he barged his way into my house." Not exactly a reminder to steady her nerves. Of course, her nerves hadn't been steady in a long, long time.

Nicky eased open the door, but Holden stopped her.

"I'm not letting you go in there," he insisted.

"They want me alive," Nicky repeated. "They'll want you dead. If anyone should go in there, it's me. But I need you…well, if something goes wrong, I need you to get the baby out."

Holden took hold of her again, and this time he didn't let go. "You're *not* going in there. Wait here. And so help me, if you disobey that order, I'll arrest you myself."

But he'd no sooner said that when someone opened the back door of the house. The place had a wraparound porch, and while the front was well lit, the back wasn't. Probably on purpose. Because Nicky saw something she didn't want to see.

Two men. A woman. And the woman had something bundled in her arms.

They didn't linger on the porch. They hurried, practically running down the porch steps.

Nicky's heart went to her knees. "They're getting away. Go after them. We have to stop them."

If Holden was listening to her, he didn't respond. He just kept watching, kept his grip on her until he finally pulled back his hand so he could send a text.

"I don't think she's holding a baby," Holden said. "I think it's a decoy."

Nicky tried to fight through the panic so she could see why he'd said that. Maybe because the bundle was huge. No way to miss that. And it wasn't anywhere near cool enough for the baby to need multiple blankets. It was September, and the temps were still close to ninety.

Plus, there was something else that was off. The woman was as tall and bulky as the two men who'd hurried *her* out of the house.

Mercy.

This was some kind of trap.

"They probably suspect we're here and will be expecting us to follow them," Holden said without taking his attention off them.

The trio got into an SUV parked behind the inn. Almost immediately, she saw the headlights of the SUV come on.

"Landon will follow them instead, and he'll have two other deputies do a quiet approach here," Holden added. "Come on. Get out of the car. Stay low and move fast. I'm going to see who's inside the house. I can't leave you here or they might try to kidnap you."

Nicky tried not to let that statement rob her of what breath she'd managed to gather. Because this was a risk. And not just the possible kidnapping. Nicky had to consider that this could be a ruse of a different kind. One where the baby was actually inside that SUV and these thugs wanted to lure Holden and her to the house.

Well, if so, it was going to work.

Of course, it was just as possible that at this very moment someone was escaping with the baby on the other side of the house. Everything inside Nicky was screaming for her to hurry.

"Do you have a gun?" he asked.

She shook her head, and he gave her one of those looks. The one that made her feel like an idiot. "I don't keep a gun in my vehicle. And besides I didn't plan on shooting anyone tonight, especially with the baby around."

"Then, what was your plan, to ask them pretty please to hand over the child?" Holden snapped.

"No. I was going to sneak in and take him. I'm pretty good at sneaking in places," she added in a mumble.

No way could he argue with that, but Nicky wished she'd had time to come up with a better plan. Too bad that thug had shown up at her house and thrown things into chaos.

"Just do everything I tell you," Holden warned her. *"Everything."*

With his gun drawn, Holden threaded them through the trees, but he stopped at the edge of the yard. There were plenty of windows, but she couldn't get a glimpse of anyone inside. However, there was another car in the small parking area on the side of the house.

She glanced back at the road and the SUV, but the trees were in the way, and Nicky couldn't tell if it actually stopped. She prayed that if the baby was indeed inside the vehicle, Landon would be able to follow them and find out where they were taking the child.

Holden led them onto the porch, and even though the door was partly open, they didn't go inside. Instead, he went to a window and peered around the edge. He snapped back so fast that she knew there had to be someone in the room. Someone who had caused his muscles to go iron-stiff.

"Two men," Holden whispered. "Both armed. There's a baby carrier on the table."

Even though she figured Holden didn't want her to move, Nicky had to see for herself.

Nicky took in everything in one quick glance.

The two men, one bald and the other wearing a black baseball-type hat.

And the ginger-haired baby asleep in the carrier.

Mercy. She'd tried to steel herself for whatever they might face, but it sickened her to think of a baby being around hired guns.

"If you create a distraction," she said, trying to make as little sound as possible, "I can sneak in."

Holden gave her a look again, to let her know that wasn't going to happen. But she didn't want to stand around there and wait. If these goons heard the other deputies, they might start a gunfight, and the baby would be caught in the middle.

Even though the window was closed, she had no trouble hearing a phone ring inside. She also had no trouble hearing one of the men answer it. Not with a greeting, either.

He simply said, "What now?"

Too bad he hadn't put it on speaker because Nicky would have liked to know who she was dealing with. But nothing. For several snail-crawling moments. She had no idea what the caller was telling him, but it caused the man's forehead to bunch up.

"All right," the man finally said. "We'll move the kid now. See you in a few." He ended the call and turned to the bald guy. "That reporter's car was just up the road. She wasn't in it, but they're sending someone to torch it and the house just in case."

Considering all the other things going on, that was small potatoes. Still, it sickened her to think of these snakes destroying her home. And it would all be for nothing. Because the files weren't even there.

"You know she didn't just leave," the other man said. "She's out there somewhere."

The first one nodded and slapped off the lights. "If she really knows what's going on, she won't shoot around the kid, and she'll make sure the marshal doesn't, either."

The thug was right about not wanting to start a gunfight, but he was wrong about her knowing what was going on. She still didn't understand why someone would do this.

"You don't shoot around the kid, either," the hat-wearing guy warned his partner. "But if you get a clean shot of the marshal, take it. Do the same to any of the locals who might show up to poke around here. Nobody who sees or could see anything gets away from here to rat us out."

Nicky's chest was already so tight that she couldn't breathe, and that didn't help. She hated that she'd involved Holden in this, and she didn't want him or anyone hurt. But the baby had to come first.

Both men started to move. Even though there wasn't much light in the room now, she saw one of them grab the carrier seat with the baby, and the other took some keys from his pocket.

Holden got them moving, too. They were quickly off the porch and headed straight for the car. The moment they reached it, he maneuvered her to the far side, away from the house, and they ducked down.

He pulled out a knife from his pocket and jammed it into the front tire and went to the rear to do the same. That would slow them down, but it wouldn't stop them. Those men were in a hurry to get out of there, and they'd drive on the rims if they had to.

The men raced out the door of the house, making a beeline for the car. They were just yards away when Nicky heard a sound she didn't want to hear.

Footsteps.

Behind Holden and her.

Holden pivoted, aiming his gun, but it was already too late.

Chapter Three

The man seemed to come out of nowhere.

Before Holden could do anything to stop him, the guy grabbed Nicky by her hair, hauled her back against his chest and jammed a gun to her head.

Damn.

This was not how Holden wanted things to play out.

He hoped there would be time to curse himself later for this botched rescue attempt. He should have waited until he had better measures in place. But maybe he could still figure out a way to fix this before it was too late for Nicky, him and, especially, the baby.

Holden scrambled to the front end of the car so he could take cover. That didn't do a darn thing to help Nicky, but he wouldn't be able to help her at all unless he stayed alive. Of course, another thug could gun him down, but right now using the car was the only option he had.

Nicky didn't stay put, either. Despite having a gun to her head, she rammed her elbow into the guy's stomach. The guy called her a couple of bad names and staggered back a step, but then latched onto her even harder.

"Try that again and I'll bash you upside the head with this gun," the thug growled.

Even though it was a clear enough warning, Nicky must have realized that he truly didn't intend to kill her. Holden could see her face tighten, could practically feel her gearing up for a fight.

"No," Holden warned her. "Don't."

And much to his surprise, Nicky listened. She also looked at Holden as if expecting him to tell her what to do next. He would.

When he figured out what the next step was.

For now, though, he didn't want her in a wrestling match with a goon who was twice her size. Just because the guy had no plans to shoot her, it didn't mean the gun wouldn't accidentally go off, and Holden couldn't risk a misfired bullet. Not just for Nicky's sake, but for the baby's.

"Can I punch her?" the thug asked his comrades approaching him.

"Not yet," the guy carrying the baby answered. "I don't want her bleeding in the car. Too hard to clean up."

His voice was ice-cold. As was his expression. He was the one wearing a baseball cap and was also the one who'd talked about torching Nicky's house and car. Holden figured he was the boss.

Well, the boss of these three anyway.

They were likely working for the person who'd been on the other end of that phone conversation. If Holden could just get the guy's phone, he might learn who that was. First, though, he had to get them out of this alive.

All three of the men were dressed in black— that was probably the reason Holden hadn't seen the third one sneaking up on them. They were all also heavily armed and wearing masks.

"Any sign of the locals?" the boss asked.

"No. But we got somebody watching the road. If they try to get here, we'll see 'em."

Holden hoped not. He hadn't made that last text sound like a life-and-death matter, but his cousin would come prepared for trouble. Which was exactly what Holden and Nicky were facing right now.

"The marshal flattened two tires," the one holding Nicky said. "What do you want me to do about that?"

"Nothing." The boss, again. He adjusted the

baby carrier in his hand so he could read a text he got. "Someone's already on the way to pick us up. They should be here any second now."

Hell. More hired guns. Just what Holden didn't need.

Holden knew he had to do something fast, but he still wasn't sure what that would be. Maybe he'd get a chance when the other car arrived. The men would no doubt look in the direction of the vehicle when it approached, and Holden could use that distraction.

Maybe.

But Landon also had to be nearby, too, and Holden had told him to do a quiet approach. Maybe his cousin would be in place before the thugs' backup arrived.

The one holding Nicky made eye contact with Holden before glancing at his partners. "You want me to go ahead and shoot the marshal?"

"No shots around the kid, remember," the boss insisted. "This is our million-dollar baby, and we can't risk it."

Even in the darkness, Holden could see Nicky's eyes widen slightly. A million bucks. That was a lot of money to pay for a baby. So, maybe this wasn't just some black-market deal.

But if it wasn't that, then what the hell was it?

Holden glanced on the other side of the car at the two men approaching, and thanks to the angle of the lights coming out of the house windows, he saw the baby then.

And he felt as if someone had slugged him.

He'd thought when he saw the kid that it would take some hard proof before he would believe the baby was Emmett and Annie's. It hadn't taken more than a glimpse. The kid was theirs, all right. The proof was all over the baby's face and that hair. However, Holden pushed aside his thoughts and concentrated on the situation directly in front of him.

"You obviously have a buyer for the baby," Nicky said. "Well, I'll match whatever offer you have. I can have the money to you within an hour."

That was probably a lie. Nicky came from money, but it would take more than an hour to gather up that much cash even if Holden was contributing. Which he would. No way did he want his nephew sold like property, and neither would anyone in his family.

He wasn't sure paying a ransom to the thugs would actually get them the baby, though. No. These men would just probably take the cash and the baby while going through with the plan to kill him. They wouldn't want to leave a marshal alive.

The boss huffed. "Save your breath, sweetheart," he said to Nicky. "I'm not gonna listen to a thing you try to tempt me with. Making a deal like that with you would get me killed the hard way."

Later, Holden would want to know what the guy meant by that, but for now he had to focus on the mess that was unfolding right in front of him. He heard the car engine. Saw the headlights, too.

And he knew this wasn't his cousin because Landon would be doing a quiet approach. In fact, Landon could already be there, but he wouldn't have let these snakes know about it.

The thugs weren't alarmed to see the black four-door pull into the parking lot and drive straight toward them.

"She goes with us," the boss said, tipping his head to Nicky. "She's got to hand over those files before we *finish* things with her. We might be able to use her father as added pressure."

That got Holden's attention. Nicky's, too. "What does my father have to do with this?" she asked.

Holden wanted to know the same thing, and he got an even worse feeling about this. Not that he needed anything else to put him on full alert.

The thug didn't answer her question, but Holden—and apparently Nicky—had no trouble filling in the blanks.

"You're planning to get that million dollars from my father," she snapped.

Bingo. Her father, Oscar, was stinking rich and would indeed pay a very high price to get his own grandson back. But there was no way a monster like Oscar Hart should raise a child. Oscar was barely a step above these thugs.

Again, the boss didn't answer. Instead, he turned to the bald guy. "As soon as we're in the car and out of firing range, go ahead and kill the marshal and torch the place."

So, this was it. Holden had to make his move.

He volleyed glances between the men and the car, but the thugs weren't looking at the car as he'd hoped. They still had their attention on Holden. That meant he'd have to wait a few more seconds until they were moving Nicky and the baby inside.

"There's no reason for you to kill the marshal," Nicky said. "In fact, if you hurt him, I'll never give you those files."

All three men stared at her. "Really?" the boss challenged. "And why would you care what happens to him? You two aren't exactly on friendly terms. Not anymore."

It shouldn't have surprised Holden that this goon knew about Nicky and him. The rumor mill was in full swing in Silver Creek, and there probably wasn't a person over the age of ten who hadn't heard about the short affair he'd had with Nicky.

Very short. As in twice.

Too bad Holden thought about those two times with her more than he did all his other relationships. Much to his disgust. He chalked up his time with her as a hard lesson learned. She was the daughter of a criminal and always would be.

"In fact," the boss went on, looking at Nicky, "the marshal might be wondering right about now if he can even trust you. He might be thinking you knew exactly what was going on before you ever convinced him to come here."

She shook her head, as if defending herself, and then she looked at Holden. "I'm not lying. Not this time. I didn't know my father was involved."

Maybe not. But she'd lied before, about her father's involvement in another crime, and that was the reason their so-called relationship had been so short. She'd put Holden in danger. His brother Drury, too.

A lot like now, in fact.

There'd been no baby involved then, but Drury certainly had been, and her lies had nearly gotten Holden's brother killed.

Holden had to tamp down the anger he still

felt just thinking about that. But Nicky no doubt saw, or maybe even felt, that anger.

The car stopped only a few yards from the men, but when the doors didn't open, the bald guy went closer and reached for the handle.

Reaching, however, was as far as he got.

Because the door flew open, fast, knocking right into the bald guy and sending him flying back. Landon barreled out of the car, his gun aimed right at the boss. But the boss only lifted the baby carrier in front of him like a shield.

There was a special place in hell for a coward like that.

Holden didn't especially need another reason to want this guy dead, but that did it. He ran toward the boss, going at him low so that he could tackle the guy. It was a risk because the baby could still be hurt, but anything he did at this point was a risk he had to take.

Nicky yelled something he didn't catch, and from the corner of his eye, Holden saw her elbow the guy in the gut again. Maybe he wouldn't shoot her, but Holden couldn't do anything about that now. He grabbed hold of the boss's legs, knocking him off balance, and the two of them went to the ground.

So did the carrier.

It didn't fall, thank God. Even now, the boss

was making sure his investment didn't get hurt, and Holden was thankful for it.

Holden didn't show the guy any such carefulness, though. He couldn't shoot him, not with the baby so close, but he could punch him, and that's what he did.

Landon scooped up the carrier and put it on the backseat. "We need to get out of here now," he warned Holden and Nicky. "We managed to steal their car, but there are at least four gunmen on the road. All of them heavily armed. They'll be on the way here by now."

Yeah, they would be, because they'd no doubt heard Nicky's shout and all the commotion.

Holden punched the boss again, the guy's head flopping back, and he raced to Nicky. He had to give it to her. For someone so outmatched, she was fighting like a wildcat, scratching and clawing the guy.

When the guy saw Holden approaching, though, he took aim at him. Holden had faced down killers before and knew without a doubt this guy would pull the trigger.

So, Holden fired first.

Nicky was about six inches shorter than her attacker, and that was just enough to give Holden a clean shot. He put a bullet in the guy's head. Before the kidnapper even dropped to the ground, Holden grabbed Nicky and ran with her to the car.

He stuffed her into the backseat next to the carrier and followed in right behind her. Holden saw his cousin Gage behind the wheel, and Landon jumped into the passenger seat.

"Hold on," Gage warned them a split second before he gunned the engine.

But Gage had barely gotten started when the shot crashed into the front windshield. Holden pushed Nicky lower onto the seat even though she was already headed in that direction, and she covered the baby with her own body. Holden covered both of them with his.

Gage sped away with the bullets still coming right at them.

Chapter Four

Nicky had so many emotions going through her. Especially fear. She had found the baby, and he was safe.

But things might not stay that way.

More shots slammed into the rear window of the car, but the glass was reinforced, and the bullets didn't make it through. Thank God. Since this was supposed to be the kidnappers' getaway car, they'd probably made sure it could withstand an attack from the cops, but Gage and Landon had turned the tables on them and had obviously managed to somehow steal the car.

"They're dropping back," Holden said. He lifted his head even more, no doubt so he could have a better look. "They're turning around to leave."

Nicky's first instinct was to say "good!" She didn't want these monsters anywhere near the baby, but there was a huge downside to that.

If they got away, she wouldn't get answers she needed as to why the kidnapping had happened in the first place.

And worse, they could regroup and come after the baby again.

A million dollars was a lot of incentive to try to kidnap the newborn and to eliminate anyone who got in their way. Plus, as long as those men were out there, they would want to get to her, too. To get their hands on those files.

From the front seat, Landon made a call, but because Nicky's heartbeat was crashing in her ears, she could only hear bits and pieces of the conversation. But she did hear him give someone their location with a request that other deputies go in pursuit of the kidnappers. He also asked that someone secure the inn. Nicky doubted the kidnappers had left any kind of evidence there, but it was a start in case the deputies didn't manage to catch the men.

"How did you get this car?" Holden asked.

"Makeshift roadblock," Gage answered, still keeping watch around them. "We parked an unmarked car sideways in the road. I hadn't planned on someone else coming in, though. I just wanted to stop someone from going out. But when the car approached, and Landon and I spotted two guys armed to the hilt, we waited until they got out of the vehicle, sneaked up on them and clubbed them."

Smart thinking. If they'd shot at the men, the others would have heard it and probably wouldn't have gotten close enough to the car for Gage and Landon to help Holden and her escape.

"The men are tied up and cuffed in a ditch," Landon added. "So even if the rest of them get away, we'll have those two. Grayson and one of the other deputies are on the way now to get them, and they'll bring them to the sheriff's office for questioning."

Nicky finally felt some relief. "Thank you. For everything."

No one acknowledged what she'd said. Maybe because they considered this part of the job. Also maybe because they didn't want to waste their breath speaking to her. She wasn't exactly on friendly terms with the Rylands even though her sister, Annie, had been married to one of them. But that connection didn't outweigh what Nicky had done.

It never would.

In their eyes, Nicky would always be the one who nearly got one of their own killed. And that was unforgivable.

"There were other men in those woods," Holden reminded them.

Landon made a sound of agreement, and there went what relief Nicky had felt. Because those men could make it to their tied-up comrades in the ditch and free them before Grayson and the others could get to them.

"We didn't want to get into a gunfight with those men patrolling the woods," Gage explained. "Because we didn't want anyone in the inn alerted. And we didn't want to risk shots hitting any of you."

Nicky whispered a thanks for that, too.

Holden had another look behind them, around them as well, and he must have been satisfied that the men weren't following them because he eased off of her. In the same motion, he looked down at the baby. Not that he could see much in the dark car, but she figured Holden had a lot of thoughts going through his head right now. She certainly did.

First things first, though—she had to make sure the baby was okay. He was squirming a little so Nicky checked to make sure he hadn't been hurt. He didn't appear to be harmed, and his diaper was even dry. He also smelled of baby formula so maybe that meant the kidnappers had taken good care of him.

That was something at least.

But there was no telling what the little guy had been through. And that broke her heart.

He'd come much too close to danger tonight. Much too close to being taken away from Nicky forever, and the threat still wasn't even over.

"Is that really Emmett and Annie's baby?" Landon suddenly asked.

"Yes," Nicky said. "I have proof from some computer files and then recordings from the clinic." Of course, that got Gage's and Landon's attention so she added, "You can't use the recordings or files to make an arrest, but one of the files identifies the baby as Emmett and Annie's son."

Landon stared back at her, and Gage even looked at her in the rearview mirror. Since they were clearly still skeptical, she huffed and tried to make this a quick explanation. Her voice was shaky. Heck, *she* was shaky, and with the adrenaline pumping through her, it was hard to think.

"I stole the information, all right," she snapped. "But if I hadn't done that and if I hadn't put a listening device in Conceptions Clinic, I wouldn't have even known the baby existed, much less found out where they were holding him."

And she wasn't going to apologize for that—especially since the info had turned out to be true and they had the baby.

"I'll want those files," Holden insisted. "The recordings and anything else you have. I don't suppose in all your snooping you also got proof of who's behind this?"

"Behind what exactly?" Gage queried.

This was probably going to be as hard for him to hear as it had been for her. Mainly because Nicky hadn't believed that anyone could do something like this.

"Someone connected to Conceptions Fertility Clinic—I don't know who, yet—used Annie and Emmett's stored embryos to make this baby. And not just him," Nicky added. "There are others. Not necessarily Annie and Emmett's child, though. In fact, I don't think it is, but there are two other newborns out there somewhere."

That got the responses she expected. A stunned look from Landon. A sound of surprise from Gage. A glare from Holden.

"Where are the other babies?" Gage asked.

"I don't know." That was the truth. "It was pure luck that I overheard them talking about Annie and Emmett's baby, and there were no other names mentioned."

"This could be connected to the missing senator, Lee Minton," Holden added after a long pause. *"Could be,"* he stressed. "But it could also be connected to Nicky's father, Oscar."

That caused both Holden and Gage to curse again, and Nicky didn't have to ask why. Her father wasn't any better liked by the Rylands than she was, and worse…he was dirty. He'd never been arrested for his shady business dealings, but that was only because he hadn't gotten caught.

Gage looked at her again in the mirror. "Oscar wanted a grandchild?"

Nicky had to nod. "Specifically, he wanted a grandson to carry on his so-called legacy."

"A daughter wouldn't do?" Landon snapped.

"My father and I are, well, estranged," she admitted. "And he wasn't exactly thrilled with Annie when she married Emmett."

"Probably because he didn't like the idea of having a federal agent for a son-in-law," Holden mumbled.

She had to add another nod to that as well. It was true. Her father hated Emmett, resented Annie for marrying him, and that's why this didn't make sense.

"It's true that my father wants an heir," Nicky continued, "but this seems…extreme considering that he hated Emmett."

"Your father does extreme things all the time," Holden reminded her. "Plenty of them illegal. Plus, if you two really are *estranged*, maybe he figured this was his only chance at having an heir from his own gene pool." Then, he shook his head. "But if he did do this, something must have gone wrong because those kidnappers said this was the million-dollar baby."

Nicky thought about that for a second. "I need to talk to my father."

"It can wait," Holden insisted. "We're almost at the sheriff's office."

She glanced out the window and saw that they were only a mile or so away, and maybe because they were so close, Landon and Holden started making preparations. Landon called the hospital and asked that a doctor come to the sheriff's office. To check out the baby, no doubt. If something was indeed wrong, though, the child would have to go to the hospital. Still might have to do that since he was obviously still a newborn.

Holden made a call, too. To his cousin Josh, who was also a Silver Creek deputy. Holden asked Josh to arrange to have some baby supplies brought in. He also asked Josh to have a CSI process the car they were driving and especially check it for a tracking device.

That got Nicky's heartbeat revving up again because she realized the kidnappers could know exactly where they'd gone. Of course, there weren't too many other places they could have taken the baby, considering that an army of kidnappers were out there.

"Are your legs steady enough to run inside while holding the baby?" Holden asked her.

Nicky nodded, prayed that was true. She wasn't anywhere near steady enough, but there was no way she'd drop the baby.

Her nephew.

He wasn't just a baby. He was her own flesh and blood.

The first time she'd heard about him on those recordings from the fertility clinic, the news had hit her like a lightning bolt. The blow didn't feel any less now that she had him in her arms.

This was Annie's son. The baby her sister had so desperately wanted that she'd gone through months and months of fertility treatments, some of them dangerous to her health. It broke Nicky's heart to know that her sister wasn't here to see the baby she'd sacrificed so much to have.

But maybe someone else had sacrificed, too.

Nicky didn't have time to bring up her concern because Gage pulled to a stop in front of the sheriff's office. Even though she'd assured Holden that she was steady enough, he still took hold of her arm as they hurried into the building.

The moment they were inside, Gage took the car to the parking lot, getting it away from the sheriff's office. Maybe because he was concerned there was something more than a tracking device in it. After all, the men had said they were going to torch her house and car so they could have been carrying some kind of accelerants.

Holden didn't stay by the door. He hurried her through the squad room and into one of the interview rooms. It wasn't especially comfortable, what with the metal table and chairs, but Nicky breathed a little easier because there weren't any windows in the room. That would make it harder for the kidnappers to come after the baby again.

Nicky sank down onto one of the chairs, but Josh and Holden stayed in the hall. They had a whispered conversation before Holden joined her, and she could tell from his expression that he was about to deliver bad news. And he did.

"The men that Gage and Landon tied up in the ditch got away," Holden said. "In fact, there are no signs of any of the kidnappers."

Nicky tried not to let that send her into a panic. Hard to do, though, and she gently pulled the baby even closer to her.

"They'll come after him again," she whispered.

"They'll try." Holden came closer, looking down at the baby. Unlike in the car, the overhead light was on, and Nicky figured he saw exactly what she was seeing.

The resemblance.

Annie's hair. But the baby's face was all Emmett.

"I've seen baby pictures of Emmett," Holden said. "That's his son."

Yes. Nicky had no doubts about that, but knowing it was just the start. They still didn't have a lot of answers.

"Obviously Conceptions Fertility Clinic was onto you," Holden continued a moment later. "That's why they sent that thug to your house. Where are the files and recordings?"

Nicky hesitated only because she'd been so terrified of the kidnappers finding them. It was the only thing she had to bargain with them in case she hadn't been able to find the baby. But now that she had her nephew—*their* nephew, she mentally corrected—there was no reason to keep them hidden.

Well, except for the sickening dread of what Holden and the others might find when they reviewed them.

She adjusted the baby's position in her arms so she could take the notepad and pen from the table and write down the storage cloud and her password. "I don't know what all the files mean," Nicky explained. "Some are just numbers and code, and I wasn't able to connect them to any names in the Conceptions database."

A muscle flickered in Holden's jaw when he took the notepad with the info. "You should have come to me or the cops the moment you found out what was going on."

"There was no time—"

"So help me," he interrupted, "you better not have withheld this because you wanted to do a story on it."

It felt as if he'd slapped her, and Nicky flinched.

More of Holden's jaw muscles flickered. "Sorry, but you don't have a good track record when it comes to this sort of thing."

No. She didn't. She'd often put the story ahead of a lot of things, including other people's safety. "I learned my lesson with your brother."

And it wasn't something she would forget anytime soon. She'd almost gotten Drury killed by withholding some evidence too long. Nicky had been working with a CPA who was helping her gather information on a crime family.

A crime family who'd done business with her father.

But the research had taken much longer than Nicky had expected. By the time she had given it to Drury, the crime family had been alerted, probably her father had, too, and Drury essentially walked into a trap. He'd nearly been killed by people he possibly could have arrested hours earlier if Nicky hadn't been digging for more.

It wouldn't do any good to tell Holden that she'd been searching for more evidence to put Drury's attackers away for life. It wouldn't do any good to tell him she was sorry. Or that she hadn't lied or withheld anything to protect her father. Sometimes, she felt as if she was drowning in the water under that particular bridge.

Holden stepped out into the hall to make a call. To his other brother, Lucas, she realized. A Texas Ranger. Holden gave him a quick update, including the cloud-storage info, and asked him to see what he could find. He then went back into the squad room for several moments.

"I wouldn't have put the baby in danger," Nicky said when Holden came back into the room. She brushed a kiss on the baby's forehead. "I'd just figured out where he was when that thug showed up at my house. And then you showed up."

With everything else going on, Nicky had forgotten about the reason Holden had come. To warn her that she was on the verge of being arrested. "Is the FBI really involved in this?" she asked.

He nodded. "Senator Minton's family hired a team of PIs to help find him. I didn't know what they found, but I got word that the FBI was looking at you as a person of interest."

Oh, mercy. She didn't need this now. "They think I had something to do with his disappearance?"

"I'm not sure. They're keeping what they have close to the vest, but now that I know what went on, I can probably stop them from taking you into custody."

"I can't go with them." She got to her feet so she could look him straight in the eyes. "Whoever hired those kidnappers had plenty of money. No doubt resources, too, to pull off a scheme like the one at Conceptions. He or she could also have a dirty cop or two on the payroll."

Holden didn't argue with that. Something that didn't help steady her nerves one bit. Even though she'd been the one to point out that particular possible danger, she'd hoped that Holden could have assured her that it wasn't likely. No way could he do that, though.

"There's one more thing," she said. "The surrogate." Nicky had to take a deep breath before she continued. "There are no surrogate names in the files, but I saw something, well, disturbing in our nephew's folder."

That got Holden's attention. He stared at her, waiting for her to continue.

"There were two notes entered on the day the surrogate delivered him. One was the location where the baby was being taken. The other was…contract terminated." Even though it'd been hours since Nicky had first seen those two words, it still gave her a jolt. "Do you think they killed her?"

Holden opened his mouth, closed it and then scrubbed his hand over his face. "Yeah."

There it was again, another jolt. Of course, Nicky had already considered it, especially after what'd gone on at the inn, but she'd held out hope. Hope that was quickly fading because the surrogate would have been a loose end. No way would the person behind this want her around so she could tell anyone about the baby she'd delivered.

Holden took out his phone again and fired off a text. "Since Grayson and the deputies are tied up here," he told Nicky, "I'll have someone in the marshals' office check and see if there have been any reports of a dead or missing woman who recently gave birth."

Nicky nodded, and even though she dreaded hearing that a woman could be dead, a woman who'd given birth to their precious nephew, they had to find out the truth. And not just about the surrogate, either.

"How will we handle the investigation into Conceptions?" she asked.

"There is no *we* in this. You aren't handling anything," he snapped, but he quickly reined in his temper.

"How are you handling it, then?" Nicky amended.

He took a deep breath first. "The other lawmen and I will have to go at it head-on. After everything that just happened, they know we're onto them so there's no need to back off. Gage is already contacting San Antonio PD and the FBI."

That meant soon Conceptions Clinic would be swarming with cops and agents. Maybe there'd be something to find, including those other babies that were out there somewhere.

She heard the footsteps in the hall, and Nicky's heart went into overdrive again, her body preparing for another threat. But it was only Landon.

"We have visitors," Landon said, not sounding too pleased about that. "The doctor's here to check the baby." Then, his attention went to Nicky. "And your father just arrived."

Nicky's stomach went to her knees. No. Not this. Not now. She was still reeling from the attack, but she also knew she had to confront him, to try to get those answers they so desperately needed.

"Why is he here?" Nicky asked. "Why did he come?" She knew it wasn't because he was worried about her, and there hadn't been time for too many people to have heard news about the attack.

Landon's gaze dropped to the baby, but he didn't have to verbally answer. That's because Nicky heard her father's voice booming through the squad room.

"Nicky, I know you're here," her father shouted. "I want you to bring me my grandson *now*!"

Chapter Five

Holden wasn't sure whose profanity was worse—his or Nicky's. She obviously wasn't looking forward to this visit any more than Holden was, and he wished he could delay it until they had more information. But he couldn't.

Because Oscar might be the very one to provide that information.

"Wait here with Nicky and the baby," Holden told Landon, and he gave Nicky a warning glance to stay put before he headed to the squad room to confront her father.

Holden passed Dr. Michelson along the way. The doc was a fixture in Silver Creek and had been taking care of the Rylands and the other townsfolk for nearly three decades, so he was someone Holden definitely trusted.

"Try to keep the baby quiet," Holden whispered to the doctor. "I don't want Oscar to know he's here. And close the door when you go into the interview room."

Dr. Michelson cast an uneasy glance over his shoulder, nodded and went into the interview room.

Holden instantly spotted Oscar when he entered the squad room. Nicky's father was still by the reception desk, and Gage was frisking him. Good. Holden doubted Oscar would come in with guns blazing. He was more the sort to hire blazing guns, but judging from the intense look on his face, anything could happen.

It'd been a while since Holden had seen the man, but Oscar hadn't changed. He was still wearing one of those pricey suits he favored. Still looked formidable despite being in his late sixties. That had something to do with his size. He was well over six feet tall and still had the body of a linebacker, which he no doubt kept toned from spending hours with a personal trainer.

"Where's Nicky?" Oscar demanded the moment he saw Holden. "And where's my grandson?"

"Your grandson?" Holden countered. Best not to show his hand until he knew exactly what hand Oscar was holding, and Holden didn't figure Oscar would just give it up.

Oscar's eyes narrowed. "Don't play innocent with me. I know they're here. Why else would the doctor be here?"

"He came for one of the deputies," Holden lied. "What makes you think Nicky is here?"

That didn't help those narrowed eyes, but Holden figured his own eyes were doing some narrowing, too. That's because Oscar had to have some kind of insider information about the attack. And the baby. He'd gotten here way too fast.

"Start talking," Holden demanded. "Don't leave out the good stuff, either, even if it incriminates you in the assorted felonies that went down tonight."

Oscar glanced around as if he expected someone to defend him. That wasn't going to happen in an office of Ryland lawmen, and the man must have figured that out right away.

"I didn't have any part in this," Oscar snarled.

"And yet you're here," Holden snarled right back. "Explain that. *Now.*"

Oscar continued to glare at him, and the glare went on for so long that Holden was ready to arrest Oscar just to let him know how serious he was about getting that explanation.

Oscar finally shook his head. "I'm not sure exactly what's going on."

Welcome to the club. "Then tell me all about the stuff you do know."

"Just tell me first if the baby is safe," Oscar ventured.

But Holden wasn't in a bargaining mood. "I'm not discussing anything else with you until I know what role you had in orchestrating this."

"I had nothing to do with it," Oscar practically shouted, and it took him a few moments to regain his composure. "This morning a package was delivered to my office. No postmark, and the courier who delivered it was gone before I knew what was in it."

"And what was that?" Holden demanded when Oscar paused.

"Photos. Some DNA results." Oscar stopped, swallowed hard. "Those bastards had my grandson."

There was plenty of concern in the man's voice, but that concern could be there because Oscar had put this sick plan into motion and then it had backfired on him.

"I want that package," Holden declared. "Call one of your lackeys and have them bring it here right now."

Oscar looked as if he might disobey that order, but he finally sent off a text. "How did Nicky know they had the baby?" Oscar asked. "Did they send her a ransom notice, too?"

"No, I found out on my own," she answered.

Holden glared at her. He didn't want her confronting her father. Not yet anyway. But at least she hadn't brought the baby out with her to do that. That meant she'd handed off the baby to Landon or the doctor before she'd come out of the interview room. Later, Holden would want to know why Landon hadn't stopped her. Then again, that was an answer he already knew. Nicky was darn pigheaded, and Landon had likely just given up on trying to hold her back.

"Where's the baby?" Oscar repeated, this time to Nicky. "Was he hurt in the attack?"

Holden latched onto that question. "What do you know about the attack?"

Oscar suddenly got very quiet. He wasn't a stupid man, but he obviously hadn't thought this visit through. Which meant he was driven by emotion. Or what substituted for emotion when it came to a man like him.

"After I got a ransom demand," Oscar finally continued, "I had my men start looking for the baby. A million dollars is a lot of money, and I wanted to make sure I actually got my grandson in exchange for the cash."

Holden groaned. "And it didn't occur to you to call the cops so they could handle this?" Like father, like daughter.

"The note in the package said if I went to the

cops, my grandson would disappear forever, that I'd never find him."

"Of course they'd say that. It's what kidnappers tell their marks nearly every time." And now that he'd given out that lecture, Holden continued. "How did you find out about the attack?"

"The ransom drop-off was to be here in Silver Creek. I was supposed to meet them fifteen minutes ago at the entrance to the park. I was there, had the money and my men in place in case something went wrong. And it apparently did."

"You bet it did." Holden motioned for him to keep going.

"I got a phone call that said there'd been a change of plans, that if I wanted my grandson and daughter to stay alive, then I'd still pay the million dollars or else they'd be attacked again. I figured you or your lawmen cousins had brought Nicky and the baby here." Oscar looked at Nicky then. "You have the baby. The kidnapper said you did, and I want him. He's my grandson."

"He's my nephew," she added.

"Mine as well," Holden said. He went to Nicky, to stand by her side.

Holden had never thought of Nicky as an ally, but in this matter, they appeared to be on the same side. Neither of them wanted Oscar to get his hands on that baby.

Oscar didn't miss the side-by-side stance that Nicky and Holden had taken. "Are you sleeping with Holden again?" Oscar asked Nicky. "Is that why he's helping you?"

Holden tapped his badge. "*That's* why I'm helping her. And as for the sleeping-with-me part, that's none of your business. In fact, you're not allowed any more questions until you answer this one, and trust me, a wrong answer will get you jail time. Are you the one who stole Annie and Emmett's embryos and had them planted in a surrogate?"

"No!" Oscar didn't hesitate, either, and if he was lying, he was doing a convincing job of it. "Something like that never crossed my mind."

"Really? Because I figured just about anything down and dirty had crossed your mind at one time or another."

That got Oscar's eyes to turn to slits again. "This isn't about me. It's about my grandson. I was willing to pay a million dollars to get him. If I'd put together this plan, I certainly wouldn't have kidnapped him."

"Not intentionally anyway," Nicky said. "But maybe the plan backfired. That happens sometimes when you hire criminals to carry out criminal activities."

Oscar cursed her, and it wasn't a mild profanity, either. Clearly, there was no love lost between father and daughter. It was also clear that Oscar did indeed want his grandson. But that didn't make him innocent in all of this.

"How soon before that package arrives?" Holden asked him.

Oscar shook his head, as if gathering his thoughts. "As soon as my assistant can retrieve it from my San Antonio office and drive it here. Maybe an hour or two."

Holden glanced back at Gage, and even though he didn't say anything to him, Gage made a phone call and asked for SAPD to escort Oscar's assistant to Silver Creek. There were two reasons for that. First, to make sure the guy actually did what he was supposed to do, and second, to keep him safe if those kidnappers decided to stop him along the way. Holden doubted the kidnappers or their boss had left anything incriminating in or on that package, but the thugs might be in the midst of tying up all possible loose ends.

Which brought Holden to his next concern. Well, a concern only because he was a lawman.

"You got a bodyguard?" Holden asked Oscar.

"Of course. He's waiting for me in the car." He tipped his head to the black limo parked just outside.

"Keep him with you. Heck, hire a couple more because if you're truly innocent, those kidnappers could come after you. Since they didn't get the million for the baby, they might make you a target instead. Or maybe they'll just put a bullet in your head because they think you know too much about their operation."

Judging from Oscar's glare, he didn't like that reminder. Or maybe he just didn't like it that Holden could be right. Oscar wasn't going to like this next part, either.

"You can leave now," Holden told him, and yes, it was another order. He wanted to get the man out of there before the baby made a sound to confirm to Oscar that the child was indeed there at the sheriff's office.

"I can't leave," Oscar argued. "Not until I see my grandson and know that he's safe."

"That's two different things," Holden argued right back. "Seeing him could put him in danger because I'd have to take you to him, and those kidnappers could follow us."

It surprised Holden when Oscar seemed to accept his answer, but he didn't accept it for long. "Soon, then. *Very* soon. I'll hire as many body-guards as it takes, but I will see him. And if you try to keep him from me, I'll get a court order."

"Good luck with that. It won't be easy to convince a judge that you have a newborn grandson when your daughter's been dead for months now. And I wouldn't count on the FBI just handing you their records of the investigation."

Oscar turned his sharp gaze on Nicky. "You know more about this than you're saying."

"That's the pot calling the kettle black," Holden said, stepping in front of her. He didn't want Nicky to start blurting out what she did and didn't know because this could be a fishing expedition on Oscar's part.

And if Nicky knew too much, or even if Oscar thought she knew too much, it could spur another attack.

"This is your last warning," Holden told Oscar. "Leave now, or I'll arrest you for obstruction of justice."

If looks could have killed, Oscar would have just sent Holden to the hereafter. "Charges like that won't stick."

"Maybe not, but at least it'll get you out of my face and behind bars for a while." That wasn't a bluff, and Oscar must have figured that out because after he belted out some more profanity, he turned and finally left.

One down, one to go. Well, one immediate to go anyway. He had a mile-long list of things to do, but it started with Nicky.

"You shouldn't have let your father know you were here," Holden told her.

"I think he already knew."

"Then you shouldn't have confirmed it," Holden amended. "Let's not give the bad guys anything else they could possibly use."

She glanced out the front windows, where her father was getting in his limo. "You really think he's behind this?"

"I'm not taking him off my suspect list." Of course, right now the only name Holden had on that list was Oscar. Oscar had means, motive and opportunity. But then again so would anyone else with a sick mind and a desire to make a boatload of money.

Since Nicky was still staring at her father's car, Holden got her moving back toward the interview room, in part because he didn't want her in front of the windows and also because he wanted to see how the baby was doing.

Soon, very soon, he'd have to deal with some major feelings stirring inside him. He'd loved Emmett, and now this baby was like having a piece of his brother. That wasn't exactly a feeling to dwell on right now, though, because it could cause him to lose focus.

Ditto for Nicky.

For whatever reason, he was still attracted to her. At least his body was anyway. But even thinking about her that way was yet another distraction that Holden didn't need.

When they got to the interview room, the doctor appeared to be finishing up his exam. Landon was holding the baby, and the doctor was putting away his stethoscope.

"He's fine," Dr. Michelson said. "Not a scratch or a bruise on him." He volleyed glances between Nicky and Holden. "Can either of you tell me what's going on?"

Since he trusted the doctor, Holden went with the simplified version. "The baby is Emmett and Annie's. We believe someone used the embryos that they'd stored at Conceptions Clinic."

Hearing the simplified version aloud gave Holden a not-so-simple jolt. Nicky had already said there were other babies, and she'd said those babies weren't Emmett and Annie's. But how did she know that?

He turned his gaze to Nicky. "Was there anything, no matter how small, in the files or the conversations you recorded to hint that one of the other babies could be our niece or nephew as well?"

She shook her head. "From what I could tell, Emmett and Annie only had two embryos stored, and both were implanted into the surrogate. But she only had one baby."

Now it was Holden who shook his head. "Why would they implant both of them?"

"That's not unusual," the doctor explained.

"They often do that with in vitro to ensure the success of getting one baby. Sometimes, even with multiple embryos, the procedure fails."

It certainly had failed once with Annie and Emmett, but it'd obviously worked with the surrogate. Holden was still caught between being furious about this whole surrogacy situation and being thrilled to still have some living part of Emmett. One thing was for sure, he loved this kid—and there was no way he was going to lose him or that part of Emmett.

"I took a DNA sample with a cheek swab," the doctor volunteered. "You want me to run it?"

Holden nodded. He didn't have any doubts that the baby was Emmett's, but he might need DNA proof in case this turned into a custody battle.

"I can tell you something about the baby," the doctor went on. "He appears to have been delivered via C-section. That's an educated guess, mind you, but his head is perfectly shaped. You don't usually see that with a vaginal birth. Plus, his birth weight seems to be a little low, maybe an indication that he was delivered before his due date."

So, they were looking for a surrogate who'd had a C-section. Possibly a dead surrogate.

The doctor motioned toward a bag on the

table as he headed toward the door. "There are diapers and bottles with premade formula. All you have to do is warm it up," he added and left.

Since Holden had more cousins than most day-care centers had employees, he figured there was someone at the Silver Creek Ranch who could tell him how to warm formula. Of course, that led him to his next question.

Where the heck was he taking Nicky and the baby?

Just thinking about it required a deep breath. "Stay in here," Holden told Nicky. She took the baby from Landon. "I'll get to work on a place for us to stay for the night."

"Us?" she asked.

Holden gave her a flat look in case she thought he was going to let her out of his sight. He wasn't. "Us," he confirmed.

Landon mumbled something about having a lot of work to do. Which he probably did. But Holden also thought his quick exit had something to do with the sudden, thick tension in the room.

"We're joined at the hip until this is resolved," Holden added to Nicky.

The corner of her mouth lifted. Not quite a smile but close to one, and it vanished as quickly as it came. "I was just thinking that you're probably not very happy about that."

"I'm not, but it should tell you just how serious I am about keeping him safe."

Him.

It was yet another reminder that they needed to work on a name, but in the grand scheme of things, it would have to wait.

"Stay here," he repeated. "I'll see if I can get an update on those kidnappers. Plus, the CSIs should be out at the inn by now."

Holden wasn't holding out hope that either would produce good results, but before he could even make it to one of the desks in the squad room, Gage was making his way toward them.

Hell.

Gage was the one Ryland who could usually put a positive spin on things, but even he was scowling.

"What now?" Holden asked.

Nicky must have heard his rough tone because she stepped into the doorway.

Gage glanced down at the paper he was holding. Paper that Holden recognized, since it was the info about the storage cloud and the password that Nicky had given him.

"It appears that about an hour ago someone erased all the files in the storage cloud," Gage said. "Everything in it is gone."

Chapter Six

Gone.

Nicky had no trouble hearing what Gage had just said, but the trouble was getting it to sink in.

"That can't be right," she insisted. She handed the baby to Holden, and she would have bolted to the squad room to find a computer to use, but both Gage and Landon stopped her.

"Your father could be watching the sheriff's office," Holden reminded her. "Or those kidnappers could be. Best not to make it easy for them to see you."

"But I need a computer," Nicky persisted.

"Wait here. I'll bring you one," Gage said, and he headed back to the squad room.

The moments crawled by. Unlike the thoughts in her head. Those thoughts were going at lightning speed. The files had to be there. They just had to be. Gage had likely just accessed the wrong account or something, and she could clear this up with a quick search.

She hoped.

Gage finally returned, and Nicky immediately took the laptop from him, sat at the table and pulled up the online storage. She put in her password. Waited.

And it felt as if her heart had actually stopped beating.

Because Gage had been right. It was empty. No files. Nothing.

Both Landon and Holden cursed, but Nicky ignored them. She logged out and logged in again, hoping it was just a glitch. It wasn't. The files weren't there even after she rebooted a fourth time.

"How could someone have done this?" Holden asked.

She was about to say she didn't know, but then Nicky remembered something critical. "Paul Barksfield. Quick, I need a phone."

Landon handed her his cell. "Who's Paul Barksfield?"

Nicky had purposely memorized his number just in case something happened to her own phone, and she pressed in the number. "He's a PI who does some work for me from time to time. I told him if something happened to me that he should make sure the files get to the cops."

"He had the password?" Holden asked, and this time his voice was loaded with suspicion.

"Yes, but I can trust Paul."

She was certain of it. But Nicky didn't like that shiver that went down her spine when the call went straight to voice mail. She left a message for Paul to call her immediately and then tried the number once more. Again, he didn't answer.

"You're sure you can trust him?" Holden asked, and Gage must have had the same question because he used the laptop to start a search.

On Paul.

"Paul's done PI work for me for nearly five years. He wouldn't have just deleted the files." She paused. "Unless he heard about the attack and thought the kidnapper might have gotten the password from me."

Of course, there were ways they could have done that—torture, drugs or some kind of coercion that would involve a threat to the baby. None were good scenarios, and Paul would have known that.

"The files could still be safe," she said, and Nicky prayed that was true. Because by now, there was probably nothing left at Conceptions Clinic that would help them unravel all of this.

"Could the kidnappers have known you gave any info to Paul?" Holden asked. The baby started to fuss a little, and he looked down at him as if he didn't have a clue what to do. Maybe he didn't, but when he started to rock the baby, he hushed.

She nearly said no, but Nicky had no idea if that was true. As she'd already pointed out, Paul had worked for her a long time, and it was possible the kidnappers had made the connection.

Judging from his expression, Landon must have thought so, too, and he took his phone back. "I'll call and have someone check on him."

Oh, mercy. That meant something could be wrong. Or more than wrong. The kidnappers could have killed him.

"Don't borrow trouble," Holden said as if he knew exactly what she was thinking. Probably because she had a panicked look on her face.

The panic continued to rise as Nicky considered who else those thugs might go after. Because of her job and her constantly being on the go, she didn't exactly have a lot of friends, and in this case that could turn out to be a good thing. Just in case, though, she needed to contact the various newspapers that often bought her stories to warn them of the possible trouble.

"We'll find Paul and get the files," Holden said. "In the meantime, we need to get the baby to a safe place. Not here," he quickly added.

"Because your father already knows you're here, and he might send his own hired thugs to try to take the baby."

That gave Nicky another slam of adrenaline that she didn't need.

"We could take them to the Silver Creek Ranch," Landon suggested.

But Nicky was already shaking her head before he even finished. "Too risky. Many of your cousins live there, and they have children."

Gage made a sound of agreement. "There are also dozens of ranch hands who could help protect you."

She still shook her head and looked at Holden. "I don't want to put another Ryland in harm's way."

"Admirable," Holden said, and there wasn't as much sarcasm in his voice as there could have been. "But whichever way we go with this, the Rylands are involved."

That meant the danger was automatic. Because they were lawmen. But that didn't mean she couldn't do something to stop them from becoming targets. Well, most of them anyway. Like her, Holden was already a target since he wasn't going to stop protecting their nephew.

"Maybe you can go to Kayla's place?" Gage suggested.

"Kayla?" Nicky asked.

"Dade's wife," Holden explained.

Dade was Gage's brother and a fellow Silver Creek deputy, but Nicky didn't know his wife.

"Kayla's, well, very rich," Gage went on, "and she has a ranch with a huge house and a lot of acreage about a half hour from here. For a while a group used it as a place for trouble teens, but it's empty now."

"The kidnappers might suspect we'd go there," Nicky pointed out.

"The Rylands own a lot of houses," Gage said, "and this one is in Kayla's maiden name. It's got a high-end security system as well as a wrought-iron fence surrounding the place. Either Landon or I could stay with you until we can come up with a real safe house."

Holden made a sound of agreement. "The house isn't far," he told her, "but it'll take us a while to get there."

Yes, because they'd have to drive around to make sure they weren't followed. It was a necessary precaution but would only add to the already long night. Not that Nicky figured she'd get any rest once they arrived at the house, but being there might be better than this limbo of waiting around for something else bad to happen.

"I'll pull a cruiser up in front of the building," Gage said.

Landon added, "And I'll get the reserve deputies that we'll need for backup. Two of them live in town so they can get here right away."

Nicky still wasn't certain of this, but then she wasn't certain of anything right now. Well, nothing except that something had to be done to protect the baby.

Holden handed her the newborn and took one of the premade formula bottles from the bag. "I'll warm this so we can feed him on the drive."

He followed his cousins, and it didn't take long, less than fifteen minutes, before Holden returned to the interview room. He scooped up the rest of the baby supplies and motioned for her to follow him. He didn't waste any time getting her into the cruiser that was just a couple of inches from the front door. Holden got in the backseat with her, and Landon was behind the wheel.

It was a good thing Holden had thought of warming up the formula because the baby started to fuss the moment Landon pulled away from the sheriff's office. Nicky had zero experience feeding a baby, but thankfully the infant took the nipple the moment she touched it to his mouth.

"The reserve deputies are behind us in an unmarked car," Landon said, glancing back at the dark blue sedan that was following them.

With the reserves, that meant there were four lawmen to protect the baby. Nicky prayed that was enough.

"Tell me everything you remember about those files you copied from the clinic and the recordings," Holden demanded.

Nicky had been expecting that demand, and Holden probably would have made it sooner if they hadn't had to deal with the aftermath of the attack. Now, though, they were dealing with the possibility that the files were lost, and if that had indeed happened, what Nicky could recall might be the only information they would have.

Not exactly a comforting thought.

"As I said, Conceptions called it the Genesis Project, and there were three files. The files didn't have names, only case numbers, but they had notes including the dates of the in vitro procedures, whether or not it was a success and then the delivery date. Except the only delivery date was for our nephew."

"Why did you hack into the Genesis Project file in the first place?" Holden asked.

"Senator Minton. I went to Conceptions, hoping to find some clues as to his disappearance, and they stonewalled me. That's when I hacked into their system and started poking around. That led me to the Genesis Project, and that in turn led me to Emmett and Annie's file."

Even now it caused her stomach to tighten into a hard knot. The last thing she'd expected to find in those files was that she had a nephew.

Holden glanced around, keeping watch just as Landon was. "Does Senator Minton have a child out there somewhere?" Holden added.

She had to shake her head. "I don't know. The notes in his file ended with the surrogate getting the in vitro procedure. It didn't say if it was successful or not. And I couldn't match his regular file at Conceptions with one of the numbers in the Genesis Project. I could only assume it was him because the dates of his wife's harvested embryos matched the ones used with the surrogate."

He took a moment, clearly processing what she'd said, and then Nicky voiced the theory that she was sure was already forming in his head. "If Senator Minton does have a child out there, and they tried to get ransom money from him, he could have refused. Or something could have gone wrong. The person behind this could have murdered him."

Holden didn't hesitate with his sound of agreement. "Or Minton could be on the run like you. Either way, Minton will need to be investigated. His wife, too."

"Beatrice," Nicky began. "I looked into her background when I was searching for her husband. She has a reputation of being a gold digger. It's his second marriage," she added. "Beatrice is the trophy wife."

"How does wife number one feel about that?"

"Her name is Dorothy, and she seems to have been glad to be rid of Minton because of all the cheating he did when they were married. The police have ruled her out as a suspect and so have I. Minton and she had been divorced for six years. No kids. Along with having a new man in her life, she's financially independent."

"Unlike Beatrice?"

"Unlike Beatrice," she confirmed. "From what I can tell, the reason Beatrice was so driven to have a child was so that she could make sure to hang on to her rich husband."

"A husband who's now missing." Holden scrubbed his hand over his face. "As soon as I can arrange it, I'll interview Beatrice."

"Good luck with that. Beatrice refused to see me."

"She'll see me because if I have to, I'll get a warrant for her arrest," Holden insisted. "Once the FBI has the info in those files, Beatrice will become a person of interest not only in her husband's disappearance, but also the Genesis Project itself."

That was true, and maybe under interrogation Beatrice would reveal something to help them with this investigation. But then Nicky had to shake her head.

"Even if Beatrice had something to do with her husband's disappearance, it doesn't explain why she would have been involved with the Genesis Project. After all, she and her husband had already gone through the process to have a baby. She was getting what she wanted."

"Maybe she wanted more. As in more money. Think about it. The person behind this was going to get a million at least from your father and probably more money from us because I doubt they had plans to hand the baby over to Oscar tonight."

True. The kidnappers could have demanded a lot more from Nicky and Holden, and unless they had found another way around it, they would have paid the ransom.

"You said there was a third file in the Genesis Project," Holden went on. "And you have no idea who that is?"

"No. I couldn't find a case that matched the reference number in the files, and it didn't have the info about the harvest date for the embryo. That could mean the clients didn't go to Conceptions, that perhaps the kidnappers got the embryo from some other facility."

Nicky figured whoever the clients were, they

must have money. Like her father, the Rylands and Senator Minton.

Holden mumbled some profanity. "I hope this isn't just the tip of the iceberg. I hope there aren't more projects like this under a different name."

Mercy, she hadn't considered that, but she should have. Anyone who would create babies only to ransom them to their loved ones had a sick enough mind to do just about anything.

"As soon as we get to Kayla's house, I'll write down everything I can remember from those files," Nicky said. Holden might be able to see something else she'd missed.

And while that was important, critical even, so was taking care of the baby.

"We'll have to stop my father from getting that court order," she said. Not exactly a news flash to Holden, but it helped her to say everything out loud. "Question Beatrice, too. I have a list of employees and former employees at Conceptions so we'll need to go over that as well."

"That's already in the works. Gage will be working on that along with anything we learn from the package that the kidnappers sent to your father."

She certainly hadn't forgotten about that or the kidnapper's car being processed, but with everything else on her mind, she'd pushed it to the back burner. The baby was on the front burner now. And not just his safety, either.

"You heated the formula," Nicky reminded Holden. "Does that mean you know how to take care of a baby?"

"Not even close," Holden mumbled.

From the front seat, Landon groaned. "I guess that means I'll be giving some instruction on diapering. Burping lessons, too. One of you will be taking the two a.m. feeding, though."

Gladly. "I want to take care of him, but I don't want to mess things up," she answered.

"Oh, he'll take care of the messing part," Landon joked. "By the way, are we going to keep calling the baby *he* or *him*? Or do you plan to give him a name?"

Nicky looked at Holden, and he shrugged. "For now we could call him Carter since that was Emmett's middle name," Holden suggested.

Both Nicky and Landon voiced their agreement, and then she looked at that precious face again. Yes, Carter suited him just fine.

With that off of her list, Nicky moved on to something else she remembered. "In the grand scheme of things," she said, "this might be minor, but I'll need to call my neighbor and ask her to take care of my cat."

Holden took out his phone and sent a text to someone. Probably Gage. Nicky was about to thank him for that, but before she could say anything, Holden's phone buzzed, and she saw Gage's name on the screen. With everything going on, he could be calling about a dozen different things, but her first thought, and fear, was that someone was following them.

Holden didn't put the call on speaker, perhaps so he could try to hide the news from her if it was indeed bad. And it was. She could tell from the way the muscles in his shoulders and arms went stiff.

"How?" Holden asked, and whatever answer Gage gave him caused Holden to mumble more profanity. "Call me back as soon as you know something."

He ended the call and put his phone away before Holden turned to her. "SAPD found Paul."

At first, she wanted to jump for joy. They'd found him, and he could explain what'd happened to those files. But that wasn't a jumping-for-joy look on Holden's face.

"Is Paul all right?" Nicky asked hesitantly, though she wasn't sure how she was able to speak. Her throat suddenly got very tight.

"No." And it took Holden a moment to continue. "The cops found Paul when they went out to his house." Another pause. "Someone shot him."

Chapter Seven

Holden read the latest text from Gage and groaned. Paul Barksfield was alive—barely. That was the good news. The bad news was that the man hadn't regained consciousness while he'd been at the hospital.

And the doctors weren't optimistic about him waking up anytime soon, either.

That meant Paul couldn't tell them who'd shot him and left him for dead. Nor could he tell them what'd happened to those files that Nicky had put in online storage. In case Paul was never able to give them that info, Holden had already moved on to the next step.

He was going through the personnel files from Conceptions.

And he was also going through the copies that Gage had sent him of the contents of the package Oscar had received from the kidnappers. The personal files had too much information. The package contents, too little. On top of which, Holden hadn't gotten much sleep and was now running on caffeine.

No wonder Landon hadn't volunteered to take the nighttime feedings.

Carter had woken up every hour, causing either Holden or Nicky to scramble to the kitchen to warm up his formula, only to have the baby take a couple of sips and then fall asleep. Around 4:00 a.m., Nicky had offered to do it on her own so that Holden could get some rest. In the massive house, that wouldn't have been a problem since it had nine bedrooms, but Holden had stayed there in the room with Nicky and Carter.

He owed his brother that much.

If their situations had been reversed, Emmett would have done the same thing for him. That would have included sleeping with the enemy. Or rather staying in the room with her.

It'd been over a year now since he'd had sex with Nicky. Holden didn't like to label them as lovers because of what'd happened afterward. Lovers made the whole thing seem too intimate. Besides, it'd been lust, that's all.

Still was.

And Holden got a full dose of that lust when Nicky came into the kitchen, where he was working. She had Carter in her arms, and the baby was fussing again. Clearly he was ready for a bottle that he wasn't going to finish, but Holden got to his feet to warm it up anyway.

"Thanks," Nicky said, sinking down onto one of the chairs at the table.

When Holden had left the bedroom about an hour earlier, both Nicky and Carter had been asleep, and he'd hoped they would stay that way for a couple of hours. No such luck, though.

Nicky yawned and after mumbling an apology, she helped herself to Holden's coffee, his cue to fix another cup. Despite the yawn, her mussed hair and the fatigue in her eyes, Holden still saw something he didn't want to see.

A damn attractive woman.

Even with no sleep or a hairbrush, Nicky was beautiful. Always had been. And that beauty had only fueled the lust when they'd first hooked up.

Was fueling it now.

Holden cursed the thought and shoved it aside. He came back to the table with both the bottle and a fresh cup of coffee. Apparently, it was exactly what both of them wanted because Carter took the bottle right off, and Nicky had some of the coffee.

"Any updates on Paul?" she asked. Her voice was tentative, as if she might not want to hear the answer.

She didn't.

But Holden gave it to her anyway. "He's still critical, still not responsive."

Nicky showed no signs of surprise about that. Probably she knew he would have come and told her if there'd been a significant change. But that lack of surprise was accompanied by some sadness and frustration.

"I'm responsible for this," she said. "Once again, I nearly got a man killed."

Holden didn't want to address what had gone on with Drury. Actually, he didn't want to address any of it, but then he saw Nicky blinking back tears.

Hell.

He hated the hole that it punched inside him at seeing her grief. Holden didn't consider himself a warm and fuzzy person, but he wasn't a jerk, either. Not most days anyway. He put his hand on her arm. Hoped that it would give her some reassurance. But no. More tear blinking.

"Paul's a PI," he offered. "He knew the risks of his job before he ever agreed to work for you."

She nodded but her body language indicated she didn't buy that at all, that she still felt this was her fault. That got him out of his chair, and because he knew it would get her mind on something else, Holden leaned down and brushed a kiss on her forehead. It probably qualified as warm and fuzzy, and it was sincere, but it caused her to give him a funny look.

That look.

Yeah, mixed with those tears was the slam of heat she'd just gotten from what should have been a chaste kiss. Apparently, nothing could be chaste between them.

Nicky avoided eye contact by staring at the baby, who had already gone back to sleep. Heck. He needed to talk to his cousins and find out how to fix this.

"Where's Landon?" she asked, looking everywhere but at him.

"Working in one of the offices. There are three in the house."

"It's a big house," Nicky agreed. She tipped her head to the stuff he had laid out on the table. "You're working, too. What is all of this?"

"Grayson emailed me copies of what was in the package the kidnappers sent to your father."

That got her attention. She shifted the baby in her arms and leaned in for a closer look.

"There's not much," Holden explained. "DNA results which may or may not belong to Carter. We won't know if it's a match for a while." And even then it wouldn't tell them much since they already knew the kidnappers had had the baby. It wasn't much of a stretch to accept they'd also done a DNA test on him.

Nicky picked up a picture of Carter. It had probably been taken only a couple of hours after he'd been born, and other than his carrier seat and the gown he was wearing, there was nothing else in the picture. That almost certainly had been by design. No way would those kidnappers have sent a photo to Oscar if it could have identified them in any way.

She put the picture aside and went to the page of typed instructions on how to deliver the ransom money. It was all to have been done as a cash drop in the park, so there wasn't even a bank account number to try and trace.

The final item she saw was a photo of a lock of Carter's hair. It was a stupid response because it was just hair, but it was a powerful reminder that if these thugs had managed to cut his hair, they could have done anything with the baby. Once Holden got his hands on them, those snakes were going to pay for this.

"Anything on the kidnappers?" she asked.

He shook his head. Holden would have considered that good news since that meant there hadn't been another attack, but in this case, out of sight was not out of mind. They were out there, and they would try to come at them again.

That's why Holden had used every security measure available at the house. Not just the internal alarms that were armed for every window and door, but also the ones for the perimeter. If the kidnappers tried to get onto the grounds, then the security system would alert them.

"And the kidnappers' car?" Nicky added. "Did the CSIs find anything?"

"Nothing useable. The car was registered to a dummy company, and it could take years to dig through all the layers to find out who owns it. By then, the company and its owner will be long gone, I'm sure."

In fact, the person was likely already gone or else had set up the account with an alias. Or even a front person.

Since Holden didn't want to keep harping on all the bad news, he turned his laptop in her direction. "I got the personnel files for Conceptions Clinic, and it's not as big of an operation as I thought it would be. A clinic manager, a medical records guy who did their computer entries, three nurses, a lab tech and two doctors. I also have the files of anyone who worked there in the past year."

Nicky put the bottle aside and scrolled through the records.

"Grayson and the others will check out each person who worked there," Holden explained. "The marshals will help with that. So will I, of course."

But Nicky didn't seem to be listening to him. She tapped one of the names on the screen.

"Amanda Monroe," Nicky said. She looked up at Holden. "I talked to her."

"When?"

"When I first started looking into Conceptions. No one at the clinic would speak to me so I asked around and found out that Amanda had once been the manager there. And she was fired."

Holden pulled up the rest of her file. Nothing about being fired in there, but then it wasn't a complete record of her employment at Conceptions. It only covered about a year. "Did she say why she was fired?"

"Amanda claimed it's because she had asked too many questions. She didn't get into specifics, though. When I pressed for details, she said she'd have to meet face-to-face, and she'd call me back to set that up. She never did, and after I found out about Carter, I didn't follow through on getting in touch with her."

Holden would do something about that. He sent a text to Grayson asking him to have someone question Amanda. The woman might have been fired because she'd learned about the illegal operation going on there.

Holden heard footsteps, and even though he knew nothing had triggered the alarm, he

still put his hand over the gun in his holster.
However, it was only Landon. At first Holden
thought he was just there to refill his coffee—
something he'd been doing ever since Holden
had gone into the kitchen—but Landon had his
phone in his hand instead of his cup.

"We might have gotten a break," Landon an-
nounced. "The CSIs at the inn found the body of
the guy Holden shot. But they also found some
blood. Not in the inn itself or by the body, but
outside in that same area where we hit one of
the kidnappers with the car door."

Holden hadn't noticed the guy bleeding, but
the door had slammed into him hard. Or maybe
one of the other men had been hurt. That was
pretty much the best option here since Holden
didn't want that blood to belong to one of the
other babies who could have been born and then
taken for ransom.

"The CSIs will try to match the DNA of the
blood they found and the DNA from the body to
someone in the system," Landon went on. "I'm
guessing those men had records. Hope so anyway. Then we can get IDs on them."

Yes, and once they had a name, they could
start looking for connections to their suspects.
Of course, right now the only suspects they
had were Oscar and Beatrice Minton. Still, this

blood was a lot more than they'd had before, and Holden would take what he could get.

"What about the safe house?" Landon asked. "Anything on that yet?"

"It'll be ready soon. I didn't want to go through normal channels since I wasn't sure who or what we were dealing with, so I'm having a friend make the arrangements."

In an ideal world, he would have wanted those kidnappers caught and behind bars before he moved Nicky and Carter again, but Holden figured it was going to be a while before anything was ideal for any of them.

Landon went closer to Nicky and glanced down at the baby. Then he glanced at Nicky and Holden. "Makes you wonder why people say 'sleeping like a baby,' huh?" The corner of his mouth lifted. "Because babies aren't especially good sleepers." Landon's half smile quickly faded, though. "So, what will happen to him after we catch the dirtbags who brought him into this world?"

Good question, but Holden didn't have a good answer. Apparently neither did Nicky.

"My father won't back down on getting custody," she said. "But neither will I. Holden and his brothers probably won't, either."

"We won't," Holden assured her, and that

meant Carter was going to be at the center of a fierce custody battle.

"Did Emmett or Annie have a will that might cover this sort of thing?" Landon asked.

Both Nicky and Holden shook their heads. Not only was there no will, Holden hadn't even had discussions with Emmett as to who would raise his future children if something happened to Annie and him. Of course, Annie and Emmett had been young, only in their early thirties, and there's no way his brother could have known that he'd have a son who would be born an orphan.

Landon made his way to the coffeepot and poured himself a fresh cup. Hesitated. "I know this is an out-there idea, but once we catch these kidnappers, you two should probably consider getting married."

Nicky choked on her own breath, and the sound caused Carter to wake up and start squirming. Holden didn't exactly choke, but he was certain Landon had lost his mind.

Landon turned back around to face them before he continued. "Oscar has a lot of money, and he probably owns a judge or two."

"He does," Nicky agreed.

Landon lifted his shoulder then, as if the rest was obvious. And it was. Oscar wouldn't back down on getting custody of his grandson, and one of the ways to possibly stop him would be for Holden to present a united front—with Nicky. Yeah, a marriage of convenience might work, but there had to be another way.

Judging from Nicky's expression, she was on the same page.

Holden's phone buzzed, and even though it was in his pocket, the sound still caused Carter to start fussing again. Nicky went over to rock him, but she didn't leave the room. Probably because she'd seen Grayson's name on his phone screen and knew this could be an update about the investigation.

Or bad news.

"Is everything okay?" Holden asked Grayson when he answered.

Grayson's slight pause let Holden know that this wasn't going to be just a simple update.

"The hospital just called," Grayson answered. "Paul's dead."

Holden couldn't help it. He groaned, and Nicky must have heard what Grayson had just said because more tears sprang to her eyes. Landon must have heard it, too, because he set his coffee aside and took the baby from her. Probably because she didn't look too steady.

"There's more," Grayson continued. "Paul

didn't die from the gunshot wound. We're still trying to work out what happened, but someone murdered him in his hospital bed."

Chapter Eight

Nicky had hoped this nightmare would end soon, but apparently it was just getting started.

Oh, God.

Paul was dead.

"He was murdered?" Landon asked the moment Holden relayed what Grayson had told him. "How?"

"Grayson's still trying to figure that out, but it appears someone injected him with something."

Nicky's breath was so thin that it took her a moment to gather enough to speak. "Wasn't there a guard or a deputy outside Paul's hospital room?"

Holden nodded. "But he was in ICU so there were a lot of doctors and nurses coming and going."

Landon cursed. "And one of those who came and went might not have been a real doctor or nurse."

Another nod from Holden. "Grayson's getting the footage from the security cameras."

Nicky heard the doubt in Holden's voice. Saw it in his eyes, too. Because someone who could have waltzed right into ICU and murdered a man probably could have tampered with the security cameras. Or worn a disguise. Heck, even if they saw his or her face, the killer was no doubt just another hired gun who they wouldn't necessarily be able to link to the person who'd hired him.

Holden shifted his gaze to her. "With Paul dead, that means you're the only person who can confirm those files ever existed."

She heard something else in his voice now. Concern. And Nicky was certain she knew why.

"The kidnappers will come after me again," she said.

Neither man denied it. But that did bring her to something she wasn't sure she wanted to consider, but she had to—for the baby's sake.

"Maybe it's a good idea to put some distance between Carter and me." Mercy, it hurt just to say those words. She'd just found him and hadn't had nearly enough time with him. "I don't want him hurt if those men manage to get to me again."

Landon made a sound of agreement. Holden didn't.

"I doubt the kidnappers are just going to give

up on taking the baby. They have a million-dollar incentive to get their hands on him again." Holden shook his head. "But it might be wise to keep Carter and you apart just so we can spread the kidnappers thin."

"They could just hire more kidnappers," Landon pointed out.

True, but Nicky was counting on that taking a while, and this way she could maybe buy Carter some time until they could catch the person responsible. Because now that person was also a killer.

Paul's killer.

Nicky squeezed her eyes shut a moment and started to pace. Holden had told her that because Paul was a PI, danger had been part of the job, but he wouldn't have been on this particular job if not for her. That ate away at her like acid. He'd died because of those files.

"Don't go off half-cocked over this," Holden warned her. "I know you want to avenge Paul's death, but we have to be smart."

Normally, she would have been offended by a warning like that. She didn't go off half-cocked. Not since the incident with Drury.

"I have to do something," she said. And apparently that something caused her to get moving. She walked out of the kitchen, not heading anywhere in particular, but Nicky just had to move.

So did Holden.

Because he caught up with her in the massive foyer by the equally massive staircase, and he stepped in front of her.

"We'll catch the person responsible for this," he said, as if it was gospel.

Nicky knew that wasn't necessarily true, but she wanted to hang on to the hope. *Had* to hang on to it.

Holden gave a heavy sigh, reached out and pulled her into his arms. She could tell from the stiffness of his muscles that this was probably the last thing he wanted to do, and she hated that he felt the need to comfort her.

Hated even more that she needed the comforting, but it was good to be in Holden's arms again. He might have thought the same thing—*might have*—because his muscles relaxed a little, and she felt a tension of a different kind.

That blasted attraction.

There wasn't time for it, and even if there had been, it wasn't something Holden wanted. Because he would never be able to trust her. Remembering that had Nicky stepping back.

At least that was the plan.

But Holden tightened his grip on her. "Swear to me that you won't do anything dangerous," he whispered.

It was another warning, one that she expected,

but that wasn't a warning tone. The attraction again, and Nicky got a full dose of that heat when she pulled back enough for their eyes to meet.

Their gazes held.

For a long time.

And during that long time, his breath hit against her mouth. Almost a kiss. With the way he was looking at her, she thought she might get a real kiss. One they'd both regret, of course, but with the need stirring in her, Nicky thought the regret might be worth it.

Holden apparently didn't, though.

He eased away from her. Oh, no. She felt a lecture coming on, but before he could tell her why a kiss or anything else wasn't going to happen, his phone buzzed again.

Another call from Grayson.

Since this could be news about Paul's murder, Nicky automatically moved closer to Holden so she could hear, but maybe he'd had enough of their closeness because he put the call on speaker.

"I have a woman on the other line," Grayson said. "Her name is Amanda Monroe, and she said she needs to speak to Nicky. Do you know who she is?"

"I do," Nicky answered. "She's the former manager at Conceptions."

"Did she say why she wanted to talk to Nicky?" Holden asked.

"No, but she says it's important. Is your phone secure?"

"It is," Holden assured him.

"Then I'll give her your number. I probably shouldn't have to remind you to record the conversation."

"No reminder needed." Holden hit the end-call button, and they waited.

Of course, time seemed to grind to a halt, and it didn't help that Nicky's imagination started to run wild. Was it a coincidence that Amanda was calling so soon after Paul's murder? Maybe. But Amanda had said she would get back to her, and maybe it had taken her this long to do it.

Even though Nicky had been anticipating the call, she still got a jolt when the buzzing sound of Holden's phone cut through the silence. He answered it and also hit a button to record the conversation.

"Nicky?" Amanda immediately said.

"I'm here. What's wrong?" She could hear the panic in the woman's voice.

"Thank God you remember me. I wasn't sure if you would."

"I remember you," Nicky confirmed. "You said you would get back in touch with me, and you didn't."

"I couldn't," Amanda explained. The woman made a hoarse sob. "I'm in so much trouble, and I need your help."

"What's wrong?" Nicky repeated at the same time that Holden said, "Is this something you should be reporting to the police?"

"Yes, I should," she said, answering Holden's question. Another sob. "But I'm not sure who I can trust because someone's trying to kill me."

Mercy. Not this. There had already been too many attacks. Especially on people who might have answers about what had gone on at Conceptions. And as the former office manager, Amanda definitely might have those answers.

"Where are you?" Holden asked the woman.

"On the way to the Silver Creek sheriff's office. I'll be there in about an hour. Can I trust you? Can I trust Nicky?"

"Yes," Holden answered. "But can we trust you?"

"Yes," Amanda responded without hesitation. "I'm not the one who tried to kill you."

There was enough emotion dripping from her voice, but Nicky knew that emotion could be faked. "Then who is trying to kill us?"

"I don't know." Another sob and then Amanda repeated those three words. "But I have some information that might help. Information that I'll only give to Nicky."

Holden rolled his eyes. "Why only her? If this is a police matter, you should be giving it to the cops."

"Because I know she's trying to make sense of all of this. That's why she called me to try to figure out what was going on at Conceptions. I want to make sense of it, too. And I want to make sure the baby is safe."

Everything inside Nicky went still. "The baby?"

"The newborn baby boy," Amanda confirmed. "I was the surrogate who gave birth to your nephew."

"AMANDA COULD BE LYING," Holden reminded Nicky again.

Nicky nodded, obviously understanding that, but that wasn't going to stop her from seeing the woman. Holden had known that from the moment he ended the call, and that's why he'd gotten started on making security arrangements.

Not exactly easy.

Not exactly foolproof, either.

Yes, Holden wanted answers as badly as Nicky, but he also didn't want this to be an opportunity for the kidnappers to come after the baby, or for the killer to come after Nicky. That's why two of his cousins, Josh and Mason, had come to the house to help guard the baby.

Landon would be staying behind with them, too, and Gage and Dade would be following Nicky and Holden to the sheriff's office.

This would tie up a lot of manpower—five deputies—so Holden only hoped Amanda would give them some information that was worth the trip.

"Too bad Amanda didn't just tell us everything over the phone," Holden grumbled as he pulled away from the house. It wasn't the first time he'd grumbled or thought that, and it wouldn't be the last.

And it wasn't as if Holden hadn't tried to have the woman fess up. He had. But Amanda had been just as adamant about having a face-to-face meeting with Nicky. Holden hoped that wasn't because Amanda was trying to lure them into the middle of another attack.

"When you first spoke to Amanda, did she mention anything about being a surrogate?" Holden asked.

Nicky quickly shook her head, and like Holden, she kept watch all around them. It was something they'd have to do on the entire trip to the sheriff's office. On the return trip as well, since someone could try to follow them back to Kayla's ranch.

Nicky made a sound to indicate she was giving his question some thought. "But if she's telling the truth about being a surrogate, that means she delivered Carter only a week ago. We might be able to tell from looking at her if she recently gave birth, especially since the doctor thought Carter had had a C-section birth."

True, but to confirm something like that meant Amanda would have to submit to a physical exam. Since Amanda didn't seem in a trusting mode, that might not happen.

Plus, there was something else bugging Holden.

"If Amanda really was a surrogate, then why would Conceptions Clinic have fired her? Why would they want to risk pissing off someone who was carrying a million-dollar baby?"

Nicky obviously processed that as well. "Maybe she wasn't actually fired. Maybe that was a front so she could take maternity leave."

And if so, that could mean Amanda might still be working for Conceptions and the person who'd orchestrated all of this. That would also mean just seeing her could be dangerous.

"If this does turn out to be a trap," Holden said, "there's a gun in the glove compartment. That doesn't mean I want to return fire," he quickly added. "But I want you to be able to protect yourself."

That caused some of the color to drain from her face. Nicky had no doubt already considered some of the bad things that could happen, but it was another thing to hear it spelled out.

Holden's phone rang, and he saw Grayson's name on the screen again. Hell. He hoped this wasn't more bad news. He put the call on speaker so that he could keep his hands free.

"No sign of Amanda yet," Grayson said. "But I just got a visitor. Beatrice Minton. She wasn't supposed to be here until later, but she said that didn't work with her schedule."

At least she'd shown up. "Has she volunteered anything?"

"Only that she's not happy that the Silver Creek lawmen seem to have a vendetta against her."

"What?" Nicky and Holden said in unison.

"Yeah. She actually used the word *vendetta* and said the interview I scheduled with her is akin to police harassment. She's a piece of work all right and seems a lot more concerned about this interview than about her missing husband."

"I want to ask her about that," Holden insisted. He wanted to ask Beatrice a lot of things including, if she knew anything about what had happened at Conceptions.

"I'll try to keep Beatrice here as long as I can so you'll get a chance to see her, but she's got her lawyer with her and I'm sure he'll advise her not to stay too long," Grayson continued. "How far out are you now?"

"About five miles from town. No one was on the road when I left the house, and I haven't spotted another vehicle."

But just saying that must have tempted fate because that's when Holden saw an SUV just ahead. Not only wasn't it moving, but it also appeared to be in a ditch.

"I'll have to call you back," he said to Grayson, and ended the call.

Holden took his gun from his holster. "It's just a precaution," he told Nicky when he heard her suck in her breath. "The person could be drunk and just have run off the road."

However, with their luck Holden figured it was just as likely to be an SUV filled with kidnappers who would start shooting at them. He prayed this trip didn't turn out to be a fatal mistake.

He slowed his car to a crawl, and behind him Gage and Dade did the same. Once Holden was closer to the SUV, he could see that the passenger window was down and that someone was inside. Not a gunman.

But a woman.

And she was slumped over the steering wheel. Holden motioned for Nicky to get down, but as she was sinking lower into the seat, she also had a look in the SUV. "That's Amanda."

He couldn't see much of her face, only the woman's brunette hair. "You're sure?"

Nicky nodded, and she touched her fingers to her mouth. "Is she dead?"

Maybe. But Holden sure as hell hoped not. There'd already been one murder. And that was more than enough. Especially if it involved a woman who could have helped them.

"Stay in the car," he told Nicky. "And call Gage and tell him what's going on."

"What *is* going on?" she asked.

"I'm going to check and see if Amanda's alive." It probably wasn't the wisest move, but if the woman was hurt, he needed to get an ambulance out here fast.

Holden waited until Nicky had finished her call with Gage before he stepped out of the car. Gage and Dade did the same, both of them drawing their weapons.

"Keep watch," Holden warned them. "This could be a setup to get to you." Of course, they likely already knew that since their gazes were firing all around them, and they were primed for an ambush.

Holden took aim at the SUV and started toward it. Slow, easy steps while he tried to listen for any sound of movement coming from inside the vehicle. He didn't hear movement, but he did hear a sound.

A moan.

Amanda lifted her head and looked at him. "Help me," she said after another moan. That's when he saw the blood on her cheek.

Holden still didn't go charging toward her. He took his time, though it was hard when she kept repeating that "help me." When he made it to the SUV, he lifted his gun, taking aim in case someone was in the back waiting to attack. But there was no one.

Amanda was alone.

And in pain.

"Call the ambulance," Holden told Gage.

Holden opened the passenger's side door and had a better look at the woman. Other than the blood on her face, there were no other visible injuries. He also didn't see any weapons, but that didn't mean there weren't any in the SUV.

"I'm Marshal Holden Ryland," he said. "And you're Amanda?"

She gave a weak nod. "Help me, please."

"Help is on the way. Tell me what happened to you."

It took her a moment and several deep breaths. "Someone ran me off the road." More of those deep breaths. "I'm not sure who it was. The car came out of nowhere."

There was a side road a few yards back, but there was no one on it now. No visible signs of damage to her SUV, either, and there was something else about this that didn't look right.

"Why didn't your air bag deploy?" Holden asked.

She lifted her head again, staring at the steering wheel as if trying to figure that out. "I don't know. Maybe it's not working."

Or maybe someone had tampered with it.

Of course, Holden had another theory about what had gone on here. Amanda had to know she was a suspect so maybe all of this had been orchestrated to throw suspicion off her.

"How long before the ambulance gets here?" she muttered.

"Not long. While you're waiting, can you answer some questions?"

She shook her head. "I didn't see who did this to me."

Yeah, he got that. "I meant questions about the baby, about Conceptions."

That caused her to pull back her shoulders, and she suddenly looked a lot more alert than she had been. "I can't talk about that yet."

"Why not?" And she'd better have a damn good reason for it.

Tears sprang to her eyes, but like the moaning and the accident, Holden wasn't sure they were genuine, either. If he was wrong about all of this, then he would owe her a huge apology, but she wasn't getting that from him now.

"I did some things, and I don't want to go to jail," she said, her voice cracking. "I need... whatever it's called."

"Immunity?" Holden asked.

"Yes. I didn't know what was going on there. I swear, I didn't know until it was too late, but I was too scared to report it. Too scared that someone would silence me for good."

Maybe. Again, he was going to withhold judgment on her innocence. "What was going on there?" he persisted.

"The babies," Amanda said after a long pause. "It was all about getting the money for the babies."

They'd already figured out that part. He needed more. "Who set all of this up?"

Amanda didn't say anything for a long time. "If I tell you, you'll have to arrest her so she doesn't come after me."

"Her?" Holden asked.

Amanda groaned, maybe from pain and

maybe because she just didn't want to say it aloud. "The woman who's behind this. Her name is Beatrice Minton."

Chapter Nine

Beatrice.

It wasn't exactly a surprise that Amanda had claimed the senator's wife was behind the things going on at Conceptions Clinic. After all, Beatrice was on Nicky and Landon's suspect list, too.

But so was Amanda.

Holden had explained the reasons why he thought Amanda's accident looked staged. No damage to her vehicle. No skid marks on the asphalt. No serious injuries. However, there were injuries—a cut to Amanda's chin and some bruises—but Nicky was hoping the doctor would be able to tell them a whole lot more once he examined the woman.

Especially be able to tell them if Amanda had indeed had a C-section recently.

"You know the drill," Holden said when

they pulled up in front of the Silver Creek sheriff's office.

Nicky did. She moved out of the car as soon as she opened the door, and Holden was right behind her. Behind him, Dade came in. He'd followed them to the sheriff's office, but Gage had gone in the ambulance with Amanda.

Along with the dispatcher, there were two other deputies in the squad room. Josh and Kara Duggan. Nicky didn't know Kara that well, but she'd heard the woman had worked for San Antonio PD before coming to Silver Creek.

Dade immediately went to his desk to get to work, but she and Holden went in search of Grayson. They found him in his office. Alone.

"Did Beatrice leave?" Holden asked.

"No. I wouldn't let her, not after you told me what Amanda said. I'm just letting her and her lawyer cool their heels in an interview room." Grayson paused. "I was also hoping you'd have more for me before I go in there. For instance, some proof that Beatrice really is guilty of something other than being a pain in the neck."

Holden had to shake his head. "No proof, and yes, I did press Amanda all the way up to the time the ambulance arrived, and she insisted that she couldn't say more until I could promise her that she wouldn't be charged with anything."

Grayson huffed and leaned back in his chair.

"It'd be nice to know what exactly she did wrong." His attention wandered to the room across the hall where Beatrice was. "But maybe Beatrice will be willing to spill something if I tell her she'd just been accused of some assorted felonies."

Nicky doubted Beatrice would say anything incriminating, not with her lawyer there to stop her, but Grayson was right. If he managed to shake her up a little, then Beatrice might tell them the pieces that Amanda was withholding.

Grayson stood, ready to go into the interview room, but then he stopped and looked at Nicky. "I'm guessing you'd like to be in there when I'm questioning Beatrice, but I need to keep this official. That means as a marshal, Holden can be in there, but you'll have to watch from the observation room. There's a two-way mirror so you'll be able to see and hear everything."

He was right. Nicky did want to be in there to face the woman who might be responsible for this nightmare, but she also didn't want to do anything that would compromise an arrest if they did manage to get enough to put Beatrice behind bars.

Grayson led her to the observation room, and Nicky immediately went to the mirror. Beatrice was there all right—pacing with her arms folded over her chest. A man in a suit was seated at the table.

Beatrice looked exactly like the photos that Nicky had seen of her. Blond hair that tumbled onto her shoulders, the curls and waves looking as if they'd each been perfectly placed. Tasteful makeup that was as flawless as the rest of her. Ditto for her clothes. In the photos with her husband, Beatrice often wore blue, probably to match her eyes, and today was no different.

When the door opened and Holden and Grayson walked in, Beatrice whirled around to face them. Or rather to glare at them.

"I've been waiting a long time," she snarled. "Need I remind you that I'm doing you a favor by coming in here to answer your idiotic questions? I guess you were too busy eating doughnuts and drinking coffee to get in here and finish this so I can go home."

Nicky could see why Grayson had called the woman a pain in the neck.

"No doughnuts or coffee," Grayson said. "Holden was waiting for an ambulance to take a woman to the hospital."

"Was it Nicky Hart?" Beatrice asked without hesitation. However, she didn't wait for an answer. "She's been hounding me for a story about my husband, and I'm fed up with her, too."

Holden took a step closer to the woman,

looked her straight in the eye. "Why would you think Nicky needed an ambulance?"

Beatrice shrugged as if the answer was obvious. "She does all those articles about criminals, crimes and such. I figure there's someone out there who might want to silence her."

A chill went through Nicky. Because it was true. Someone did want to silence her for good. Was that someone Beatrice? If so, Beatrice wasn't doing much to cover up her guilt. Maybe because there was no guilt for her to cover up.

"It wasn't Nicky who was hurt," Holden continued a moment later. "It was Amanda Monroe."

That got a reaction from Beatrice. Her eyes widened. "The office manager from Conceptions Fertility Clinic?"

"That's the one," Grayson said. "What do you know about her?"

Beatrice actually seemed surprised by the question, as if it was the last thing she'd expected they would want to know. So maybe this wasn't Beatrice's attempt to cover her involvement after all.

"I don't actually know her," Beatrice answered. "The only time I met her was when she was still working at the clinic. She did the initial paperwork when Lee and I went in to start the process for my egg harvesting." She paused. "How was she hurt? *Why* was she hurt?"

Holden went even closer, violating the woman's personal space. "You tell me. Amanda said you're the one behind her attack."

Beatrice dropped back a step, and she volleyed some stunned glances between Grayson and Holden. "Amanda said…?" But she stopped and made a sound of outrage. "I had nothing to do with anything that happened to her." She jammed her thumb against her chest. "I'm the victim here."

Her lawyer practically jumped to his feet and reached out for her, but Beatrice slapped his hand away. "I'm the victim," she repeated. "And I won't be treated like a criminal when I've done nothing wrong."

She no longer had that pain-in-the-neck tone or glare. Beatrice sank down onto one of the chairs and buried her face in her hands for a moment.

"We need to talk before you say anything else," her lawyer insisted.

"She needs to talk now," Holden argued. "Someone ran Amanda off the road, and Nicky was nearly killed. I want answers about that."

Beatrice shook her head. "I don't know if what happened to me is even connected to them."

Grayson went closer to the woman, too.

"Then tell us what did happen, and we'll figure out if it's connected or not."

"Mrs. Minton," the lawyer said, his voice a warning for her to stay quiet.

But it was a warning she ignored. "Lee and I went to Conceptions Fertility Clinic about a year and a half ago. I desperately wanted a baby and had been unable to get pregnant. I went through all the egg harvestings, all the procedures, but I still wasn't able to conceive. Lee said we had to stop trying…that it was putting too much strain on our marriage."

"Was it?" Holden asked, and Nicky was thankful he had because she wanted to hear the answer, too.

Beatrice shrugged. Then her eyes narrowed a little after she paused. "This stays here in this room, and you'd better not breathe a word of it to anyone else." Despite the fact that neither Holden nor Grayson agreed to that, she continued. "Lee was having an affair, and that was putting far more strain on our marriage than my trying to have our baby, his heir."

She spat out the last two words like venom. Clearly, Beatrice was not a happy wife.

"Who was he having an affair with?" Grayson asked.

"The latest one is some bimbo ex-beauty queen. Sharon Bachman."

Nicky knew the name and had heard the rumors linking Sharon to the senator. But then, several other names had come up, too. Apparently, Lee had a roving eye. Of course, Beatrice had known that when she married him because he'd cheated on his first wife with Beatrice.

"Do you think Sharon had anything to do with your husband's disappearance?" Holden continued.

"Maybe," Beatrice readily admitted. "The two could have run off together. I suspect he'll turn up when he realizes what a mess he's made of things. Well, I'm not taking him back this time. I won't be treated like dirt again."

The woman certainly had a lot of anger, but if what she was saying was all true, then Nicky could understand that anger. Well, except for the fact that Beatrice had made her own bed by cheating with a cheater.

"There's more," Beatrice said a moment later. The lawyer tried to stop her again, but Beatrice gave him a stern look of her own. "I have to tell someone, and it might as well be them."

"What do you have to tell us?" Holden prompted when Nicky didn't continue.

She took a few more moments, some deep breaths as well. "A couple of days after my husband went missing, I got a call. The voice sounded mechanical, like it was a computer speaking. Anyway, he said that Lee and I had a son. One that'd been born using a surrogate, and that if I wanted the baby, I was going to have to pay a million dollars to get him."

Oh, mercy.

That put the knot back in Nicky's stomach. That was the same thing that'd happened to her father. Of course, it didn't mean Beatrice was telling the truth, but there were tears in the woman's eyes now.

"I told the caller that I didn't believe him," Beatrice went on. "And he said he had proof. DNA proof. He claimed that they'd implanted my embryo into a surrogate, and that she'd given birth to our child."

"And you believed that?" Grayson asked.

"Not at first, but then I got this package with photos of the baby, and I knew that was my son." Her voice was trembling now. So was Beatrice. Or at least she was pretending to tremble. "They said if I went to the cops that I wouldn't see the baby so I went to Lee's financial manager and begged him for the money. My name's not on Lee's accounts so I couldn't just take it. He finally gave it to me, and I arranged to pay the ransom."

Holden cursed. "That was risky and stupid. You could have been killed. That's why people take matters like this to the cops."

"I know that now." A hoarse sob tore from her throat. "I dropped off the money in a park just like the kidnapper asked, but they demanded more. A half a million more." She looked at Holden, and while she was blinking hard, as if trying to stave off tears, there weren't any actual tears in her eyes.

"Did you pay it?" Holden asked.

She nodded. "Again, I had to beg Lee's financial manager, and he told me that it was all I was going to get, not a penny more. He went with me that time to pay the ransom." Beatrice paused. "And we got the baby."

Nicky didn't know who looked more surprised by that—Grayson, Holden or her.

"Where's the baby now?" Holden demanded.

"At one of Lee's estates. I hired three bodyguards to stay with him so I could come here, but that's why I'm so anxious to get back to him. I'm afraid someone will try to take him."

That could happen despite the fact the kidnappers had gotten a million and a half out of the deal. They could want more. In fact, that could have been their plan all along, to continue to get as much as possible from the birth parents.

However, hearing all of this reminded Nicky of something she'd read when she had been researching the senator, and while Grayson probably wasn't going to like the interruption, Nicky went to the interview room and tapped on the door.

Holden was the one to open it, and yes, she'd been right about Grayson not liking this. He shot her a scowl, but maybe the scowl would ease up when he heard what she had to say.

"Beatrice signed a prenup agreement," Nicky whispered to Holden. But obviously she didn't whisper it softly enough because Beatrice got to her feet again.

"So?" Beatrice challenged.

Nicky hadn't intended on spelling this out herself, but now everyone had their eyes on her. "So, if your husband divorces you or even if he dies, you won't get any of his money or properties."

Nicky had been guessing about the dying part, but judging from the way Beatrice's chin came up, she'd been right about that.

"What are you implying?" Beatrice snapped.

Since Nicky had already opened this particular box, she emptied the rest of the contents. "That maybe you arranged for the surrogate to have the baby. Then you set up the kidnapping so that you could milk money from your husband's accounts."

The flash of temper went through Beatrice's eyes, and she moved as if to launch herself at

Nicky. The lawyer intervened, stepping between them, but he had to take hold of Beatrice's shoulders to stop her.

"If you repeat that to anyone, I'll sue you for everything you have," Beatrice warned her.

"Are you saying you didn't arrange for your own son's birth and then *kidnapping*?" Holden asked. Unlike Beatrice, his voice was calm. So was he, and that seemed to agitate Beatrice even more.

"I'm not saying anything else to any of you." Beatrice snatched up her purse. "This interview is over."

"Think again," Grayson said. "You just admitted to a participation in a crime."

"A crime where I was the victim!" Beatrice fired back.

"A crime where your son was the victim," Holden amended. "You didn't report that crime to the police, and by doing that you concealed critical information in a federal investigation."

Grayson nodded. "You're not going anywhere until we get a full written statement about what happened," he added. "Even then you might not be leaving anytime soon. The faster you cooperate, the faster you might get out of here. *Might*."

The lawyer didn't argue with that, which meant he knew his client had just dug herself a massive legal hole. But it wouldn't necessarily lead to Beatrice's arrest because if the woman was telling the truth about all of this, she'd done what any normal person would have done to get her baby.

"I'll take her statement," Grayson said to Holden. "Why don't Nicky and you head on out?"

"Remember what I said about suing you," Beatrice snarled when Nicky and Holden turned to leave. "I will if you say a word about this to anyone."

It wasn't even worth her breath for Nicky to respond. Nor did she have time. That's because the moment they were in the hall, Holden's phone buzzed, and she saw Gage's name on the screen.

"How's Amanda?" Holden asked. He put the call on speaker, but he didn't do that until after they were out of earshot of Beatrice.

"I'm not sure. Amanda's lawyer showed up, and he won't let us talk to her. The doctor wanted to keep her overnight for observation, but after she found out a man had been murdered here earlier, she insisted on being transferred to a hospital in San Antonio."

Nicky couldn't blame the woman for not wanting to stay there, but it could also be part of some ploy to make her look innocent. Because if Amanda was indeed the one behind this, then she would have been responsible for that murder.

"I'll go with her to make sure she doesn't try to run or do something stupid," Gage continued. "How'd it go with Beatrice?"

"She claims that kidnappers had her son. A son born under the same circumstances as Carter."

"Claims?" Gage repeated, unable to hide the skepticism in his voice.

"Yeah. Grayson's with her now, and I'm hoping he can sort out the truth. Maybe you can do the same thing with Amanda when her lawyer lets you talk to her."

"Funny thing about that—the lawyer's not going to let that happen. But Amanda did hint that she'd be willing to talk to Nicky and you. Any chance you two can get to the hospital before she's moved?"

Holden groaned, and Nicky knew that was the last place he wanted her. However, it was the one place where they might learn whatever role Amanda played in all of this.

"We can go there now," Nicky said.

It took Holden a moment before he agreed. He ended the call, his attention immediately going to Kara, probably because his two cousins were on the phone.

"I need backup while I go to the hospital with Nicky," Holden told her.

Kara nodded, called out to the others that she was leaving, but Holden had them wait inside until he went to the parking lot and drove a cruiser directly in front of the door. The moment they were in the cruiser, he didn't waste any time driving away.

"You think Beatrice was telling the truth about anything?" Holden asked her.

"Yes, about the affair. About taking the money from her husband's account, too. But remember, there was nothing in the files about a surrogate being successfully implanted with the Minton's baby." Nicky paused. "That doesn't mean it didn't happen, though."

"And it doesn't mean that Beatrice wasn't the one behind it," Holden added. "This way, she could get the money, an heir to the Minton fortune, and she wouldn't have to ruin her figure to do it."

Yes, Beatrice seemed vain enough for that to have been a consideration.

"We need to find out what happened to her husband," Nicky said, thinking out loud. Of course, plenty of people had been searching for the senator for over two weeks now, and there was still no sign of him.

Maybe for a reason.

"You believe that Beatrice could have murdered him?" Nicky asked.

"I do." Since Holden didn't hesitate, it meant his mind was already going in that direction. "Beatrice could have killed him because of the affairs, but then hidden his body until she had the money she could get from his estate."

True, but Nicky had to shake her head. "With a Minton heir, she'd get the entire estate anyway."

"Yeah, but it would likely have conditions attached. Minton probably has a will where he named a trustee to control any heir's accounts. That could mean Beatrice wouldn't have been able to touch the money for herself."

Nicky had to agree with that, and it meant they had some more digging to do. This was where she could help since she'd already established contact with a lot of the senator's family and friends. If there was dirt to dish on Beatrice, one of them might do it.

Holden pulled into the parking lot, slowly, and looked around. "I'll pull up to the door again," he instructed. "You two get out and stay in the waiting room while I park."

He turned in the lane to do just that when Nicky felt the jolt. It was as if someone had shot out one of the tires, but she certainly hadn't heard a gunshot. But it didn't take long, only a couple of seconds, before she heard something.

A blast.

And it ripped through the cruiser.

HOLDEN HADN'T SEEN what had caused the blast, but he'd certainly heard it.

It was deafening. He felt it, too, because the blast lifted the front end of the cruiser off the ground and then slammed it back down again.

Nicky, Kara and Holden were all wearing their seat belts, thank God, but that didn't stop them from being slung around like rag dolls.

Holden's shoulder slammed into the steering wheel, and the pain stabbed through him. So hard that he thought he saw stars. But he fought through that and checked on Nicky and Kara in the backseat. Both women looked dazed, but they didn't seem to have any injuries.

But that might not last.

Holden got a glimpse of something he darn sure didn't want to see. It was one of those ski-mask-wearing thugs like the one who had attacked them the day before. The guy was armed, and he was crouched down behind a car. He didn't stay crouched for long, however. He started running toward the cruiser.

"On your left," Holden warned Kara.

The deputy was moving slowly, but she'd already drawn her gun. She pivoted in that direction now, and Holden was about to do the same when something else caught his eye. Something that sent his heart into overdrive.

A second gunman.

This one was coming at them from the other side.

"Stay down," Holden warned Nicky, but that was only a temporary measure.

Holden hit the locks on the doors just as the first shot blasted into the window next to Kara. The glass was bullet-resistant, but that didn't mean bullets wouldn't eventually get through. And the gunman was trying to make that happen sooner rather than later. He started firing nonstop at the window.

And he wasn't doing that alone.

The other guy started shooting at Holden's window.

Holden tried to get the cruiser moving, but the explosion had disabled the engine in addition to putting a big crater in the concrete in front of them. He threw the cruiser into Reverse and tried again.

Nothing.

"I'm calling for backup," Kara said, taking out her phone.

Good. But even though the sheriff's office

was just up the street, Grayson might not be able to get there fast enough.

"Gage is inside the hospital," Holden reminded Kara, and the deputy immediately called him.

"He's on the way out," Kara said a moment later, though it was hard to hear what she was saying. Both gunmen were continuing to rip apart the glass in the windows.

"If they get through, you stop the one on your side," Holden told the deputy. "Don't let him get to Nicky."

Because he would kill her.

This wasn't a kidnapping attempt. These men wanted her dead. Or at least their boss did, and he or she had paid them to commit murder.

"I need a gun," Nicky insisted.

Holden got her one out of the glove compartment, though he hated the idea of her having to shoot to protect herself. He and Kara were in law enforcement so it was different for them. This was their job. But as a reporter, Nicky hadn't signed on for a gunfight in the middle of a parking lot.

In the distance Holden heard sirens. A welcome sound, but he saw something else that would help, too.

Gage.

His cousin was skulking around some cars, coming toward them. Holden only hoped the gunmen didn't see him first because unlike the thugs, Gage wasn't wearing body armor.

Holden had to do something to make sure Gage didn't get shot while trying to help them. He lowered his window, just enough to stick out the barrel of his gun, and he took aim at the gunman. Well, he took aim as best he could considering he had no room to maneuver. He also had to be careful. He couldn't just fire off a random shot because it might hit an innocent bystander. He waited until he had the best shot he thought he might get.

And Holden fired.

His shot hit the guy in the chest. Of course, the Kevlar was protecting him from a kill shot, but he staggered back and stopped firing.

Holden knew it wouldn't last, knew he only had a couple of seconds at most before the gunman regained his balance. Holden adjusted his aim. Fired again.

This time Holden didn't shoot him in the chest. But rather in the head.

The guy went down like a rock.

Holden pivoted to try to do the same to the second man, but Gage was already in position. The thug probably didn't even see Gage since his focus was on his shots, which were eating their way through the window. And he succeeded.

The bullet came crashing through the cruiser.

Holden yelled for Nicky and Kara to get down. They did, but he couldn't tell if either were hit. That's because the shooter left cover to come in for the kill.

Big mistake.

Gage left cover, too.

The thug saw him at the last moment, and he pivoted in that direction. But Gage got off the shot he needed. No shot to the chest. This one went into the guy's head, and like his comrade, he fell to the ground.

Holden felt a split second of relief. But it didn't last. That's because he looked in the backseat to check on Kara and Nicky.

And that's when he saw the blood.

Chapter Ten

"It's just a cut," Nicky said.

She wasn't sure how many more times she'd have to remind Holden of that before it sank in. Or got that troubled expression off his face. He had the look of a man who'd just made a huge mistake.

And he might indeed see it that way.

Nicky saw it differently. They were all alive, and the only injury had happened when the gunman's bullet had sliced across Nicky's arm. It'd stung like fire then. Still did. However, she didn't want Holden to see any signs of her pain because he was already beating himself up enough about this.

"All done," the nurse told them when she finished the stitches and placed a bandage over it. "The doctor's writing a script for some pain meds—"

"No need," Nicky interrupted. She didn't

want them—not just for Holden's sake, but also because she didn't want a fuzzy mind. There were too many things about this investigation they still had to work out.

The nurse glanced between Holden and her as if waiting for Nicky to change her mind about those meds. "Okay, then I'll get your paperwork so you can leave."

"Could you make it fast?" Nicky asked. "I have some things I want to check on."

The nurse shrugged, mumbled that she would see what she could do and walked out, leaving Holden and her alone in the treatment room. Nicky immediately got up and would have started out, too, but Holden stepped in front of her.

"You were just shot," he snarled.

"No, I was just grazed. I'm fine, and I want to talk to Amanda before she leaves."

Holden didn't budge. He just stared at her. Then, he reached out, put his fingertips on the bandage and used his thumb to measure the distance between the graze and her heart.

"Three inches," he said, "and that bullet could have killed you."

"Yes, but it didn't."

He looked down at the space and must have realized that his thumb was not only over her heart, but was also on her breast. She expected him to jerk back his hand, and he did move it, but Holden did it slowly. In the same motion, he lowered his head.

And he kissed her.

Nicky wasn't sure who was more surprised by the kiss, but the sound she made got trapped between their mouths. This wasn't some little peck of comfort, either. Holden kissed the right way, and he eased his arm around her, inching her closer to him.

He was careful with her arm. Careful with her. Treating her as if she was fragile glass that might shatter in his hands. She wasn't sure how he could manage to deepen the kiss with such a soft touch, but he did it. When he finally pulled away from her, Nicky wasn't just breathless. She was plenty aroused.

Hardly the right time for it since they were in the ER.

"I'm sorry about you getting shot," Holden said. "I'm not sorry about the kiss, though."

Yes, he was, because he groaned right after the words had left his mouth.

"It's okay," Nicky assured him. "It doesn't have to mean anything."

That was a lie. It did mean something, and it broke down barriers that she needed in place to protect her heart. Obviously, all the danger had made her a little crazy because she was already thinking about what it would be like to land in bed with Holden again.

Oh, yes, she was definitely a little crazy.

And maybe it'd done the same thing to Holden.

As if to prove that it didn't have to mean anything—or to disprove it—he pulled her back to him. In the same motion, his mouth came to hers for another kiss. This meant something all right. It was deeper than the other one, and there wasn't a hint of sympathy in it.

It was pure heat.

It didn't stay just a kiss, either. Holden pulled her closer and closer to him until they were body-to-body. Pressed together in all the right places. Or rather the wrong places, since it fired up that heat even more.

Being in his arms brought back all the old memories. Of the time when they'd been lovers. Hard to forget something that amazing, but they were clearly making new memories, too. Ones that Holden might not want to be making with her.

That didn't stop him, though.

He staggered back, taking her with him, and he landed against the wall. She landed against him. Her breasts against his chest. Against his hand, too. That's because Holden slipped his hand between them and cupped her breast while he took those clever kisses to her neck.

She melted and forgot all about the gunshot. The pain. Heck, she forgot how to breathe.

Nicky figured at any second he would come to his senses and stop this. He didn't. The kiss raged on until she felt it in every part of her body. Until she was the one who was grappling to pull him closer.

Until she was thinking that sex was a possibility.

It wasn't.

Nicky repeated that to herself several times, but it didn't sink in until Holden finally pulled back, and she could see the apology in his eyes. An apology that was about to make it to his mouth.

"Don't say you're sorry," she told him.

He stared at her. A long time. "We don't need this right now. Agreed?"

She nodded. Easy to agree to that considering they'd just been attacked. "Will it help if we agree?" she asked.

"Not at all," he drawled. "Still, I have to try."

Nicky had to nod at that, too. They did have to try, but she figured they both knew they were failing big-time. They'd just made out in a hospital ER so there wasn't much chance of resisting each other if they ever got some time alone.

Thankfully, that probably wouldn't happen anytime soon. Then, when this was over, she could stand back and assess whatever the heck she was going to do about these wildfire feelings she had for Holden.

"You're sure you're up to seeing Amanda?" Holden asked.

Good. They were moving on to something they should be doing. Even though her body disagreed with that.

"Of course I want to see her." That was possibly a lie, too. She wasn't up to seeing anyone right now except Holden and Carter, but Amanda might tell Nicky things that she wouldn't tell the cops.

Holden stared at her as if trying to decide whether to call her on that lie or not. He didn't. "This way," he finally said, and he started with her down the hall.

Nicky spotted two uniformed guards, one at each end, and she figured there were other guards and deputies posted around the building. The explosion had happened just yards from the entrance, and security was going to be tight.

"Nothing on the dead guys yet. They had no IDs on them," Holden said. "I got an update while you were getting a shot to numb your arm for the stitches."

Yes, she'd heard him just on the other side of

the curtain, but Nicky hadn't been able to make out much of the conversation.

"Their prints should be in the system, though," he added a moment later. "So, once Grayson has those, we'll probably get a match."

Good. That was the first step in figuring out who hired them.

But Holden wasn't acting as if that was good news.

"Is something wrong?" Nicky finally asked.

"Your father found out about the attack. And he knew you'd been hurt. He called Grayson before you were even examined."

"How did he find out?" However, Nicky waved off the question. Waved and then flinched when she felt the pain in her arm. Obviously, the numbing meds were already wearing off.

Holden noticed the flinch all right, she thought. He cursed. And the muscles in his jaw got very tight again. Best to get his focus back on the investigation rather than her injury.

"What did my father say to Grayson?" she asked.

That tightened his muscles even more. "Oscar says he'll use this to get custody of the baby, that it's not safe for Carter to be around you because someone's trying to kill you."

Nicky wished she could argue with that, but

it was true. Still, that didn't mean her father should have the child.

"Grayson's going to call Oscar and tell him to back off, that the baby is in protective custody," Holden added. "*My* protective custody."

She doubted that would get her father to back down even a little, but it was better than nothing. Plus, it was good to know they had Grayson on their side.

"The safe house is ready," Holden added. "I got a call about that, too."

Again, Holden didn't make it sound as if that was good. Probably because they still had to get Carter there, and with the threat seemingly all around them, that might not be easy to do.

"But we got some bad news on the blood that the CSIs found at the inn," Holden explained a moment later. "No match."

Nicky shook her head. "That doesn't make sense. Those men who attacked us almost certainly had records." She froze. "Oh, God. You don't think it could have belonged to a baby?"

"No," he said immediately. "There's no evidence that there was another baby in that place. It probably just means we wounded the one gunman who wasn't in the system."

Yeah, the odds were against that. Well, maybe. Maybe whoever was behind this hadn't hired the usual thugs to do thug work.

They continued to another hall, where Nicky saw yet another guard. This one was outside one of the hospital room doors, and as they got closer, she spotted Gage just inside the room. With Amanda and a tall lanky man. Her lawyer, no doubt.

"The doctor decided to release her," Gage volunteered. "She won't be transferred to another hospital after all."

Amanda was dressed not in a gown but in regular clothes, and she was sitting on the edge of the bed. "As soon as the paperwork is done, I'm leaving. I would have already left, but if I do, the doctor said my insurance wouldn't cover any of this."

So, Nicky apparently wasn't the only one caught in the red-tape maze today.

"Gage said you'd been shot," Amanda continued.

"Grazed," Nicky explained. "It's nothing, really."

Amanda shook her head. "It is something. It means someone tried to kill you just like they tried to kill me."

Nicky hadn't made up her mind yet if that last part was true or not. She went closer to the woman.

"Will you tell me how you became a surrogate for my nephew?" Nicky asked.

Silence.

"Amanda already knows she's a person of interest in this case," Gage said.

"I'm innocent," she snapped. "I became a surrogate because I needed the money. I didn't know until afterward what was going on."

"And when exactly did you learn what was going on?" Holden asked. He, too, went closer.

More silence.

It caused both Holden and Gage to huff.

Since Nicky wasn't sure how much time there'd be before that paperwork was done, she asked the one question she desperately wanted Amanda to answer. "Who set all of this up?"

Amanda's exhaled breath was long and weary. "I don't know. But I can tell you who it wasn't. It wasn't me. If I'd just gotten all that ransom money, do you think I'd be worried about insurance paperwork?"

She would if she wanted to add to the facade of being an innocent woman.

"Then guess who's behind it," Holden persisted.

"Beatrice," Amanda readily answered. "But I've already told you that." She paused, looked at Nicky. "And your father, of course."

Nicky felt her heart thud. Not because Amanda had mentioned her father, but because the woman had added that *of course*.

"Why my father?" Nicky asked.

Amanda made a sound as if the answer was obvious. "When I was still the manager there, he came to Conceptions several times. He made a pest of himself by demanding to know what procedures we were doing on his daughter. I told him I couldn't give out that kind of information. The man was obsessed with having a grandchild."

Yes, he was, and it obviously didn't seem to matter that he'd resented Annie for marrying Emmett. Or maybe Oscar had simply decided that he didn't care about his feelings for his daughter as long as he got that heir he wanted.

"Annie died ten months ago," Nicky reminded Holden, "and the in vitro would have been done on the surrogate—on Amanda—just a month later. Maybe less."

He nodded. "You think your father was so racked with grief that he did this and then covered it up with the ransom demand."

"It's possible."

"But I wasn't the only surrogate," Amanda blurted out. Her hand flew over her mouth, and it was obvious she hadn't intended to spill that.

Even though Nicky knew there'd been others, at least two of them since she had seen the files, what Amanda said gave her a very uneasy feeling.

"Emmett and Annie don't have another baby out there, do they?" Nicky asked.

Amanda frantically shook her head. "I've already said too much."

No, she hadn't said what Nicky needed to hear. One of those three in vitro procedures was still unaccounted for.

"Please," Nicky said to the woman. "I just need to know if I have another niece or nephew because he or she could be in grave danger."

More head shaking from Amanda. "I can't help you."

"Can't or won't?" Holden snapped.

"Can't," Amanda answered. "I honestly don't know anything about a third baby. Heck, I don't know much about my own delivery. They put me to sleep during the C-section, and when I woke up, the baby was already gone. They took him without even letting me see him."

"That's all my client intends to say," the lawyer said. "And you'll have to leave now. You're agitating her."

"A baby's life could be at stake," Nicky insisted.

But Amanda just lowered her head. No eye contact. Nothing.

"Sheriff Ryland will expect you to bring your client in for questioning," Holden told the lawyer. "Or for her to surrender for an arrest."

"I'll be at the sheriff's office in the morning," Amanda said, her voice a raw whisper. "Just make sure you have enough cops there to protect me. Because a baby isn't the only one at risk. We all are."

For once they could agree on something, and as much as Nicky wanted to be at Amanda's interrogation, she was betting that Holden wasn't going to let her out of the house.

"Let's go," Holden told Nicky, and he put his hand on her back to get her moving.

"By some miracle you don't remember anything else about that third file, do you?" he asked once they were in the hall and away from Amanda's room.

"No, and that's why I need to find out what happened to those files." That gave Nicky another wave of grief and guilt over Paul's murder.

"Is there any place where Paul could have stored them so he knew you'd find them?" Holden asked.

Nicky gave that some thought. "We worked together many times so I guess he could have put the info in some of his old case files."

That prompted Holden to take out his phone and make a call. Not to Grayson this time. But to Drury. Holden didn't put the call on speaker, but judging from what she could hear of the conversation, Drury was going to get started on that process.

"Paul probably had a lot of case files," she reminded Holden when he finished the call. "He'd been a PI for over twenty years."

A search would be a needle in a haystack. Still, it wasn't as if they had a lot of leads at the moment. And the search was now more pressing than it had been. The file had said that both of Annie's embryos had been implanted into a surrogate, but maybe there had been two surrogates and not just one.

It turned Nicky's stomach to think of another baby being out there—any baby—but this third child might also be Emmett an Annie's.

With that thought eating away at her, she and Holden made their way back to the ER, where Nicky hoped her release paperwork would be waiting for her. If not, she was going to ask Holden if they could leave anyway. She figured she wouldn't get him to agree to that.

Until she saw who was waiting for them in the treatment room where she'd gotten her stitches. Not the doctor or the nurse.

But rather Beatrice.

Holden automatically stepped in front of Nicky, and he put his hand over his gun. Beatrice's eyes widened for a second, but then the glare came.

"Really?" the woman snapped. "You think I'd come here to attack you?"

Holden tipped his head toward the parking lot. "Considering what happened out there, I'm not taking any chances."

Beatrice added a huff to her glare. "I'm here to help you, and this is the thanks I get."

"What kind of help?" Holden asked, and his tone was one of a lawman questioning a hostile suspect. Beatrice qualified as both.

"First, I need your assurances that you won't bother me or my son any further."

"No deal." Holden didn't hesitate, either. "You're a suspect in not only what happened at Conceptions Clinic, but also your husband's disappearance."

"And I've already told you I'm innocent of both," she snapped. Beatrice shifted her attention to Nicky. "I understand Amanda is hospitalized here."

Nicky only lifted her shoulder and didn't intend to verify that. She wasn't sure what Beatrice would do with the info.

However, Holden had something to say. "Where's your lawyer?"

"In the car waiting for me. Why?"

"I just wanted to make sure he wasn't sneaking around trying to find Amanda and putting together another attack. Nicky and I have had our fill of bullets being fired at us."

"Fine, be that way. Believe what you will," Beatrice continued, her voice a snarl now. "But I know Amanda's here, and I know the things she's been saying about me. She's the reason you suspect that I might have done those horrible things. Well, I have proof that I didn't."

"I'd be very interested in that proof," Holden assured her.

Even after making the claim of having something to clear her name, Beatrice looked as if she was still debating what to do. She finally reached in her purse, a move that had Holden drawing his gun.

"I don't carry a weapon," Beatrice spat out.

Holden didn't holster his gun. He kept it aimed at her until they saw what Beatrice took from her purse. It was a flash drive. She didn't hand it to them, though. She just lifted it for them to see.

"What is that?" Nicky finally asked.

"Proof. It's the surveillance footage of me paying the ransom to get my son."

Of all the things that Nicky had been expecting the woman to say, that wasn't one of them. Judging from the way he pulled back his shoulders, Holden was surprised, too. Or maybe he was just skeptical.

"How did you get footage like that?" Holden demanded.

"After things went wrong with the first kidnapping demand, I hired a PI, and he did surveillance not only of the park before the ransom drop, but also during and afterward."

Now it was Nicky who was skeptical. "The kidnappers didn't notice they were being recorded?"

"No." But then Beatrice paused. "Or they didn't seem to notice."

That was the key word here, *seem*. Whoever was paying those kidnappers had set up a complex operation with a lot of security in place. It seemed strange that they wouldn't check for someone filming them. Of course, if the kidnappers were wearing ski masks, maybe they didn't care since they couldn't be identified.

Nicky shook her head. "Why didn't you give this to the cops?"

"Because those monsters who brought me the baby said for me to stay quiet or they'd kill me and take the child." Her breath was rapid now, and she looked away. "But now that so many people know what went on at Conceptions Clinic, I'm worried my son and I are in danger whether I talk or not."

Holden took a moment, no doubt to process that comment, since that's what Nicky was doing. "How would a surveillance tape of a ransom drop prove you're innocent?" Holden asked.

Beatrice took Nicky's hand and put the flash drive in her palm. "Just watch it, and you'll see who's really responsible for all of this."

Chapter Eleven

Holden put the flash drive in his laptop and watched as the info popped onto the screen. There was only one file, and it was indeed a video. However, that didn't mean Beatrice was right about Nicky and him seeing the person who was responsible for the Genesis Project and the kidnappings.

"The images could be doctored," Holden reminded Nicky, though he doubted she needed such a reminder.

After all, Beatrice was still a suspect and whatever was on the footage could be there simply to clear her name. Holden seriously doubted that the woman would have given them anything to incriminate herself. Just the opposite.

Nicky nodded, her attention already nailed to the screen, but Holden didn't miss that her forehead was bunched up. "Are you in pain?" he asked.

"No." But Nicky must have realized she said it too quickly because she flexed her eyebrows. "Just a little."

Translation—she was hurting *bad*. It didn't matter that the bullet had only grazed her— she had five stitches, and the area around those stitches was no doubt throbbing.

Even though the footage was already loading, he hit the pause button, and went to the bathroom off the master suite. While he was there, Holden checked on the baby and Landon—both were napping so he didn't disturb them. He went back into the kitchen with a bottle of over-the-counter painkillers and got her a glass of water.

It was a testament to how much Nicky truly was hurting because she didn't argue with him about taking the meds. While he was at it, he sent a text to Gage so he could contact the doctor to write Nicky that prescription for pain meds that she'd turned down earlier.

"I'm okay, really," she said after she took the pills and set both the bottle and the water on the kitchen table.

Holden went closer. In fact, he got right in her face, and he stared at her.

"All right, I'll be okay once the painkillers kick in," she admitted.

Holden sighed, eased her onto one of the

chairs and, because he thought they both could use it, he leaned down and kissed her.

"You keep doing that," she whispered against his mouth.

"Yeah. Want me to stop?"

The corner of her mouth lifted. "Only because we should be reviewing the video."

Holden certainly hadn't forgotten about it, but he silently cursed the distraction. And it wasn't even Nicky's fault. It was his own. His body had the notion that Nicky was his for the taking.

And she wasn't.

He sank down beside her and got the footage moving. As he'd expected, the quality sucked. It was nighttime, and the PI had obviously shot from a distance. Probably an attempt to stop the kidnappers from seeing him. The problem was Holden couldn't see the kidnappers. Or Beatrice, for that matter.

"You recognize that part of the park?" Nicky asked.

Holden nodded. "It's a trail that coils around the creek." Not exactly on the beaten path, which was why the kidnappers had likely chosen it.

He fast-forwarded it until he saw the headlights come into view. Since the vehicle was a limo, Holden figured this was Beatrice. It was.

The woman stepped out several moments later, and she had her lawyer right by her side.

She was also wearing a Kevlar vest.

Hardly her usual attire, but Holden was a little surprised that she would have remembered to wear body armor. Most parents of kidnapped children were in a panicked state by this point, and their own safety was usually the last of their concerns.

What Beatrice was missing was the money. Neither she nor her lawyer was carrying a bag, and that probably meant the ransom was inside the vehicle.

Thanks to some moonlight, Holden could see Beatrice look around. He could also see the moment she stepped even farther behind her lawyer. That's because a second vehicle approached. An SUV, and it pulled close enough that the front bumper butted against the front bumper of the limo. From that angle, Holden couldn't see a license plate, but even if he could have, the plates probably would have been bogus.

Two men barreled out of the SUV. Both of them were wearing ski masks, just as Holden had figured they would be. They were also armed, and the sight of those armed thugs sent Beatrice scurrying back into her limo.

"No audio," Nicky mumbled when they

watched as one of the thugs appeared to shout something.

That was too bad, but Holden figured he'd ordered Beatrice out of the car because the woman came out, finally, and she clutched on to her lawyer. It was the lawyer and the shouting thug who did all the talking, and it was only a few seconds before the lawyer leaned into the limo and came out with two huge bags.

No doubt the ransom.

With Beatrice still cowering by the limo, the lawyer came forward, and he put the bags of money on the ground for the kidnapper to inspect. The guy riffled through both, and then motioned to someone in the SUV. It didn't take long for another kidnapper to get out.

And he was holding a baby.

The exchange happened fast. The kidnapper with the baby took him to the lawyer, practically thrusting the infant into his arms. In the same motion, the other kidnappers grabbed the bags with the money.

Beatrice and the lawyer didn't waste any time getting the heck out of there. The moment the lawyer was behind the wheel, he took off.

The SUV didn't.

Holden was about to say that there'd been nothing on that footage that had proven Beatrice was innocent. She could have been faking the fear. Faking everything if those kidnappers were actually working for her.

But then Holden saw something.

When the kidnappers opened the back passenger door, the moonlight hit just right for him to see the person sitting there. And judging from Nicky's gasp, she had no trouble seeing it, either.

Because it was her father.

She staggered to her feet, catching onto the chair for support. Since she still didn't look too steady, Holden looped his arm around her, mindful of her injury. Also mindful that this had knocked the breath out of her.

"I knew he was dirty," she said, "but this?"

Yeah, Holden was right there with her. It was sick enough to create a project to produce your own heir, but here Oscar had done it to Senator Minton and milked him for a million dollars.

Well, maybe.

Holden shook his head. "Why would your father have risked going to the ransom drop?" The question was for himself more than Nicky, and he was trying to piece this together. "I mean, there are three hired guns so why would he have gone knowing that something could have gone wrong?"

"You think he was set up?" Nicky asked.

His initial reaction was to say "heck, no," but

that's because it was hard to think of Oscar as anything but a criminal. However, Oscar wasn't stupid, and this was a stupid thing to do.

Unless…

"Maybe Oscar didn't trust his hired guns." But there was a problem with that theory, too. "How much do you think your father's estate is worth?"

"Millions. And I haven't heard of him losing a large sum with investments and such. In fact, if anything, he's only added to his fortune with his shady business deals."

Holden gave that some more thought, knowing that the thinking would have to end fast and that he would have to call Grayson to tell him about this. Of course, these were the same questions Grayson would need to ask as well.

"Is there a personal connection between your father and Lee Minton?" Holden added.

"Nothing obvious. I checked for that when I first learned about the Genesis Project. The only thing they had in common was the embryos stored at Conceptions Clinic."

If Oscar didn't have a grudge against Minton and since he didn't appear to need the money, maybe Oscar had orchestrated this for a different reason. To throw suspicion off himself. After all, he could claim he'd been forced to pay a million dollars as well to get his grandson.

There was only one way to find out for sure.

He took out his phone and called Oscar. Part of Holden didn't expect the man to answer, but he did on the first ring.

"I want my grandson," Oscar snarled before Holden could even say anything. Obviously, he'd seen Holden's name on the caller ID.

"I want a lot of things," Holden countered. "Like the truth. Is there something you want to tell me?"

Considering that Holden hadn't given the man much of a clue as to what he was looking for, it didn't surprise him that Oscar hesitated. But the hesitation went on for several long moments.

"The only thing that matters now is getting my grandson," Oscar finally said. "I heard about the other attack, and I don't want him in the middle of that. The court order is in the works, and I'll have custody of him by tomorrow."

Probably not.

"If you're telling the truth about wanting your grandson out of danger, maybe you can just stop the attacks," Holden suggested.

Another hesitation. "If you've got something to say to me, then just come out and say it."

Holden considered it a moment and thought about just waiting until he had Oscar in front of him. But the sooner he could get this information, the better. Then he could bring in

Oscar not just to interrogate him, but also to arrest him. Since there was no bail for a murder charge, it would get Oscar off the streets and perhaps put an end to the danger.

"Well?" Oscar taunted. "Cat got your tongue?"

"No. I thought you'd like to know that Beatrice had a PI film her ransom drop with the kidnappers," Holden finally said.

Silence. For a very long time. "I think I should call my lawyer now."

"I think you should, too. You should call your lawyer and show up with him at the sheriff's office in one hour."

That wouldn't give Holden much time to set up the interview and go over the charges with Grayson, but it also wouldn't give Oscar much time to go after Nicky again.

"Be there," Holden ordered. "Because if you're not, I will send someone to arrest you."

With that, Holden hung up and immediately called Grayson. While he was explaining things, he emailed Grayson a copy of the surveillance footage. Grayson agreed that both Oscar and Beatrice needed to be brought in for another round of questioning, and Holden wanted to be there for that.

"What about Nicky?" Grayson asked. "Are you going to leave her at the house when you come here?"

Nicky was obviously close enough to hear that question because she started shaking her head. Even though Holden didn't like this, he was actually going to agree with her.

"I think we need to keep the baby separate from Nicky," Holden explained. "Starting now. I'll bring her with me to the sheriff's office, and Landon and the reserve deputies can go ahead and take the baby to the safe house."

Grayson made a sound of agreement. "I'll get Kara out there now to drive in with you. The reserve deputies, too, to go with Landon."

Holden figured Kara might not be too happy about that considering she'd been attacked earlier because of them. And Grayson likely didn't want her out on a call so soon afterward. But what with everything going on, Grayson's deputies were probably all tied up. That would continue because Landon and the reserve deputies would have to stay at the safe house indefinitely with Carter. Although *indefinitely* might not be that long.

"This is the right thing to do," Nicky said as if trying to convince herself.

She turned, making her way to the master suite with Holden following right behind her. Yeah, it was the right thing to do, but he didn't feel good about this. In a way it felt as if he was abandoning his brother's son. Of course, this was temporary, and if the interviews with Beatrice and Oscar went well, then Carter might not have to stay in the safe house for long.

And then what?

The question wasn't out of the blue exactly. Holden had been thinking about what the next step would be. A step that would no doubt include a custody battle unless they could put Oscar behind bars. Even then, he and Nicky might square off since both could make a case for a claim to the baby.

Nicky seemed unaware of the emotional battle that was going on inside Holden. That was probably because she was having her own battle, and by the time they made it to the bedroom, she was blinking back tears.

"I know Carter hasn't been in our lives for long," she said, "but in a way, it feels as if he's always been here."

Holden felt the same way, and it crushed his heart to say goodbye.

Landon sat up when they walked in, and he glanced at both of them. "Time for me to take him to the safe house?" Landon asked.

Holden nodded, not trusting his voice. There was a lump in his throat.

Nicky went to the bassinet ahead of Holden, and she leaned down and kissed Carter on the cheek. The baby stirred but went right back to sleep. Holden waited a moment before he, too, gave the baby a kiss.

Nicky got busy packing up the baby's things, probably to give herself something to do. Holden decided to try that ploy as well, and he headed back toward the kitchen to warm up a bottle. However, he didn't get far into the process when his phone buzzed, and he saw Grayson's name on the screen.

Hell. He hoped nothing else had gone wrong.

"Please tell me there's not a problem," Holden said when he answered.

But Grayson didn't jump to respond to that. "As soon as Kara arrives, I need you here at the sheriff's office."

Holden groaned. Yeah, there was a problem all right. "Why? What happened?"

"A detective from San Antonio PD just called. They've been going through Paul's business records, and they think they found something. They're emailing it to me now."

Holden went still. "What did they find?"

"Information about the Genesis Project." Grayson paused. "Get here as fast as you can."

Chapter Twelve

For Nicky it seemed to take an eternity for Holden, Kara and her to make the drive to the sheriff's office. However, saying goodbye to Carter had gone by as fast as a blink of an eye. Maybe he wouldn't have to be in that safe house for long.

Because there could be something in Paul's files to put an end to this.

Grayson hadn't gotten into the details over the phone, mainly because he was waiting for the emails to arrive from SAPD, but when she and Holden finally arrived and hurried back to his office, Grayson had those emailed documents printed out and spread on top of his desk.

"What did they find?" Nicky couldn't ask the question fast enough.

"This." Grayson moved one of the papers for her to have a look.

It was Paul's handwritten notes for a case

where she'd hired him to interview some witnesses to an old unsolved murder. Since that murder had happened on the other side of the state, Nicky wasn't sure how it connected to what was going on now.

She shook her head. "This was the last case Paul worked for me before Conceptions." But she stopped the head shaking when she saw the note at the bottom. Paul had added the address for a website.

Grayson turned his laptop for her to see. "The site was for online storage, and I used your password from the other site to access it."

Nicky went closer, and she saw the files that she'd copied from Conceptions. "Why would Paul have moved them?" she asked.

Grayson lifted his shoulder. "Maybe because he knew the other site had been compromised or had the chance of being compromised. He probably knew that eventually you'd see the note and realize what it was."

Holden went closer, too. "Are all the files there?"

Nicky scrolled through and nodded, then she froze. Yes, all her files were there, but there was also another file that Paul had created. There were lots of notes and what appeared to be test results, but like the other files she'd copied from

Conceptions, this one didn't have names, only a file number. She looked up at Grayson to see if he knew about it.

He did.

Grayson cleared his throat. "According to Paul, there's a third baby."

Mercy. Of course, she'd known all along this was possible, but there was something in Grayson's expression that warned her there was more to this than just a third baby.

Holden must have picked up on it, too, because he stepped in front of her and almost frantically scrolled through what Paul had left them. Specifically, it was another file that he'd apparently gotten from Conceptions.

Paul had written, "The computer geek I hired managed to recover this from the clinic's files before it was erased for good." And he'd written that note on the same day he'd been murdered.

That explained why he hadn't told her what he'd found.

But what exactly had he found?

Holden kept scrolling, and when Nicky saw Paul's other notes, her breath vanished.

"The other baby is Emmett and Annie's," Holden said. "And it's a girl."

The blood rushed to Nicky's head, and before the panic could hit her, she kept searching for information in Paul's notes. And there was more.

"Payment requested," she said, reading the note.

But that was it. Paul hadn't written anything else, and Nicky's gaze snapped to Grayson's for answers. Answers that he clearly didn't have because he shook his head.

"Your father is in the interview room just across the hall," Grayson said. "Beatrice should be here any minute, and I'll get Amanda back in here as well."

Nicky tried to make sense of this, but like everything else in this case, she couldn't make sense because of the slam of emotion. There was a baby out there. Somewhere. Her niece. And someone had apparently requested payment for her.

But what did that mean?

Did it mean she'd been sold on the black market? And if so, who'd bought her?

"You think Amanda might have delivered twins?" Grayson asked.

"That's one of the things I intend to find out," Holden insisted. He looked at Nicky. "I would tell you to let Grayson and me handle this, but I'm figuring you'll want to talk to your father."

"I do," she insisted, and Nicky stormed toward the interview room.

Grayson was right behind her. Holden, too, and they were both mumbling some profanity. Maybe because more had just been added to this nightmare, but it might also be because they were worried she was going to compromise the investigation. And she prayed she didn't, but she needed answers now.

She threw open the interview room door, and her father and his lawyer immediately got to their feet. Her father didn't sling one of his usual barbs at her. Perhaps because he saw the raw emotion on her face. The anger as well.

"Start talking," she demanded.

She expected him to stonewall her or hide behind his lawyer, and to stop him from doing that, Nicky charged toward him. She didn't push him against the wall—something she desperately wanted to do —but she did go toe-to-toe with him.

"Why were you in that kidnapper's SUV, and where is Annie and Emmett's daughter?"

Her father had opened his mouth, maybe to answer some part of that, but he went silent. His eyes widened, and he shook his head.

"A daughter?" he asked, his voice mostly breath and almost no sound.

He certainly acted surprised, but Nicky wasn't ready to buy in to that surprise just yet. "Yes. Now, tell me where she is."

Her father shook his head again and looked at Holden as if he expected him to make some sense of this.

"If the file is right, someone paid for her," Holden explained. "Maybe a ransom, maybe just payment from the person who arranged for her to be born. And I'm thinking that person is you."

"No," Oscar said. He stepped around Nicky and went to one of the chairs. He tilted back his head, sucked in some long breaths. "The only baby I knew about is their son."

Nicky went to the table so she could look him in the eyes. "But you were in the kidnappers' SUV. We have proof."

"So-called proof that you got from Beatrice," the lawyer said.

Oscar motioned for him to get quiet, something that surprised Nicky. But then maybe her father had done that because it would make him look innocent.

"I was in the SUV because the kidnappers took me at gunpoint," her father said. "They made me go to that ransom drop and told me if anything went wrong that they'd set me up to take the blame for it."

Nicky went through each word, hoping she could see a flaw in what he was saying, but she had to admit that it could be true. *Could be.*

"There's really another baby?" Oscar asked.

Holden stepped forward to answer. "According to some information we just learned, yes. Now, where is she?"

Her father gave a weary sigh, followed by a groan. "I told you that I don't know, and those men never once mentioned another child. If they had, I would have arranged to pay a ransom for her, too."

"You're sure?" Nicky snapped. "Or maybe because she was a girl, you decided one male heir was enough."

Oscar shifted his gaze to her. "I would have paid the ransom," he repeated, and it was the most convincing thing he'd said since this whole ordeal had started.

"Are you sure the kidnappers didn't mention anything about another baby?" Grayson asked.

"Positive. Trust me, I would have remembered something like that. They kept me blindfolded and put headphones on me until we got to the ransom drop. I didn't see or hear anything that would help me identify who they were or if they had another baby."

"How did the kidnappers get to you?" Holden pressed.

Oscar gave another weary sigh. "I wasn't being careful enough. After I got that package and knew I had a grandson, I hurried out of my San Antonio office to go to the bank. They grabbed me in the parking lot."

Holden jumped right on that. "Were there security cameras in the parking lot?"

Oscar scrubbed his hand over his face. "No. They malfunctioned or something."

Nicky was betting it was the *or something*. The kidnappers had probably disabled it before they even took her father. That didn't mean he was innocent, though, because they could have done that on his orders so that no one could analyze it to disprove it was an actual kidnapping.

But even if Oscar had set up all of that, it didn't mean he knew of the newborn baby girl.

"I have a theory," Nicky said to him. "You wanted an heir so after Annie died, you paid someone at Conceptions Clinic, maybe Amanda, to carry Annie and Emmett's child. But someone decided a good way to make some money would be to have a second child, another million-dollar baby. Except this time, you'd actually have to pay the million to get her."

"Your theory is wrong," her father spat out, and it earned her one of his harshest glares. "If that had happened, why hasn't someone contacted me by now? There have been no other ransom demands."

"Yes, there has been," someone said.

Beatrice.

She was in the hall, and it appeared that Josh had been escorting her to an interview room. Clearly, she'd heard at least part of their conversation, and she got everyone's attention.

"What do you mean?" Holden snapped.

"I mean I just got a call on the way over here, just minutes ago, and the kidnappers said there was another child. A newborn girl. And that if I wanted her, I'd need to pay another ransom."

"That doesn't make sense," Nicky said. "Why would the kidnappers contact you? Did they say the child was yours?"

Beatrice flinched. "I, uh, just assumed that she was, that the kidnappers had implanted one of my embryos into another surrogate. I have six of them stored at Conceptions."

And maybe they had used one of Beatrice's for this child. Maybe the baby didn't belong to Emmett and Annie after all.

But then why had Paul thought it was theirs?

There was also the problem with the payment requested. Paul would have copied that file days ago. So, did that mean the kidnappers had requested payment from someone else? Like her father. And that he'd refused? Or had the file been wrong altogether?

Nicky looked at Holden to see what his take was on this, but he only shook his head. "Come on. Grayson needs to finish this interview with your father."

Yes, and maybe Oscar would say something that would shed some light on what the heck was going on. In the meantime, though, Nicky wanted to get to work on finding the third baby. That started with Beatrice.

Holden and Nicky went into the hall with the woman, and they followed Josh and Beatrice into the other interview room.

"I recorded the call," Beatrice volunteered, handing Holden her phone. "I don't usually do that, but after what happened with my son, I do. I've also hired several more bodyguards for him." She shuddered. "God, I'm so scared someone's going to try to take him again."

Nicky knew how she felt. Or at least how the woman was pretending to feel. Beatrice wasn't off the suspect list just yet.

Holden hit the play button on the call, and it didn't take long before Nicky heard the voices. First, Beatrice answering, and then the man's voice. It was muffled as if he was trying to disguise it.

"Mrs. Minton, guess what I'm holding right now?" The caller didn't wait for her to answer.

"A cute little newborn girl. She looks just like her twin brother. If you want her, it'll cost you another million. Get the money by tonight, and I'll be back in touch with you."

That was it. The man hadn't given Beatrice a chance to say anything.

"I'm not sure I can get the money," Beatrice said. There were tears in her eyes now. "I mean, I had to beg for the last ransom." She looked up at Holden. "But you think this might not even be my child?"

"We're just not sure. It's possible the kidnappers will try to get additional ransoms from both Oscar and you."

Mercy, that would be a huge haul of cash. And the problem? They just might succeed, especially if they managed to get their hands on Carter and the Minton boy again.

"So, what do I do?" Beatrice asked.

Nicky didn't have the answer, and even Holden hesitated. "We'll monitor your phone and will tell you what to say when the kidnapper calls back."

Beatrice didn't look very comforted about that. "Should I demand DNA proof like what they gave me with my son?"

"Don't make any demands. In fact, don't say anything to them until we instruct you." Holden turned to Josh after Beatrice nodded and then walked out into the hall.

"Wait," Josh told the woman. "I'll stay with you."

Beatrice moved away from the door, but judging from the sound of her footsteps, she didn't go far.

"You've got experience with this sort of thing from your FBI days?" Holden asked.

Josh nodded. "I'll find a place to set up the drop. You think you'll be able to tell if the baby is Emmett's if you have a photo of her?"

"Maybe. The kidnapper did say she looked like her brother. He could have been lying."

True. In fact, all of this could be a lie. There might not even be another baby, and the person who'd put this plan together could have added that fake file so he or she could get more money.

"I feel like I'm on an emotional roller coaster," Nicky said.

But before she even got out the words, Holden was already putting his arm around her. He eased her to him and brushed a kiss on her forehead. Josh would have been blind not to notice, and he did notice all right. She saw just the flash of disdain in his eyes.

Disdain because of what'd happened to Drury, no doubt.

Since that was something Nicky could never

escape with the Rylands, she backed away. Or she would have if Holden hadn't kept his arm around her.

"You're not the only one on that roller coaster," Holden assured her, and he kept her there in his arms. "It might be a little while before I can take you back to the house," he added. "Everyone's tied up at the moment."

They were, and what with everything they'd just learned, the being tied up might last for a while.

"I'd like to go through Paul's files some more," Nicky said. "The files I got from Conceptions, too. There could be something in them I missed."

And even if there wasn't, she had to do something. Anything. The nerves were raw and right at the surface, and if she didn't get busy, she might break down and cry again. That wouldn't help Carter, this possible baby or anyone else.

She and Holden went back to Grayson's office, but they'd barely made it inside when Holden's phone buzzed. With all the bad news they'd gotten, Nicky's muscles tensed. Then, they did more than tense when it hit her that something could have gone wrong with getting the baby to the safe house.

Her gaze flew to Holden's phone screen, but

it wasn't Landon's name there. However, it was a name she recognized.

Amanda.

Holden answered right away, no doubt ready to start firing off questions to the woman about the third baby, but Amanda spoke before he could say a word.

"You have to help me," Amanda insisted. She sounded out of breath. Sounded as if she was also crying. "Please. You have to get here right away."

"Where are you and what's wrong?" Holden asked.

"I was at the inn just up the street, and my lawyer went out to get something. Oh, God." Amanda was definitely crying. Sobbing, actually. "Please, come. Someone broke in to my room. I climbed out the window and ran, but he's chasing me."

Holden cursed. "Who broke in? The kidnappers?"

"No." Another sob. "I only got a glimpse of his face, but I'm pretty sure it's Senator Lee Minton."

Chapter Thirteen

Holden wasn't sure he was doing the right thing, but either way he went with this could be dangerous for Nicky.

Amanda could have lied to get Nicky and him out into the open again. But the lie could have merely been to get some of the cops out of the building so it'd be easier for the kidnappers to have another go at killing them. There'd been attacks at the Silver Creek sheriff's office before, and he wouldn't have put it past Amanda—or whoever was behind this—to try to orchestrate another one.

Holden already had his gun drawn and ready, but he had no idea if Amanda was even coming their way. Josh and Kara had responded immediately, heading to the inn to see if they could spot Amanda. Spot the person who was chasing her, too.

If that person existed, that is.

"Just stay back," Holden reminded Nicky when he saw her peering out the doorway of Grayson's office.

She nodded. "You really believe Minton broke in to Amanda's room?" Nicky asked.

"I don't know."

But Beatrice must have heard Nicky mention her husband's name because she came running out of the interview room.

"You found Lee?" she asked.

"Don't get your hopes up," Holden told her. "It might not be the senator at all." Or in Beatrice's case, maybe it was a hopeful situation because she might not want her husband to be found.

"What's going on?" Beatrice demanded, and she started to charge forward, but Nicky caught onto her arm, not only holding back the woman, but also filling her in on what they knew.

Which wasn't much.

"As soon as the deputies find Amanda, she'll be able to tell us what happened," Holden added to Beatrice when Nicky had finished. Whether or not Amanda would be telling them the truth was a different matter.

"Amanda had a C-section a little over a week ago," Nicky added. "She probably won't be able to get far."

Yeah, that was the good and bad news. The

woman probably wasn't going to be able to run for long, if at all, but that meant if this was a real attack, Amanda could already be dead.

Holden decided to keep that to himself.

Beatrice took out her phone and frantically pressed in some numbers. "I'm trying to call Lee. I've been trying ever since he went missing, but his phone was turned off and the card was taken out so it couldn't be traced. But maybe his phone is working now."

It was a serious long shot, but Holden preferred Beatrice to be doing something other than pestering him. If possible, something that would also get her away from Nicky. Beatrice wouldn't have made it through the metal detector to get into the building if she'd been carrying a weapon, but that didn't mean she couldn't signal some thugs to attack.

"Go back in the interview room," Holden ordered the woman.

But Beatrice didn't move. She seemed frozen. "Lee?" she said when someone apparently answered her call. "Oh, God. It is really you?"

Holden hoped like the devil that this wasn't some kind of trick, but since the senator's body had never been found and there'd been no signs of foul play, it was indeed possible that he was still alive. But how had Minton gotten mixed up in all of this?

"Lee wants to talk to you," Beatrice said. She walked toward Holden, her hand shaking while she held out the phone.

"Put it on speaker," Holden instructed, and he stayed near the door. Keeping watch. "Nicky, get Grayson."

Nicky nodded and hurried across the hall to do that, and it only took a couple of seconds for Grayson to tell her father and his lawyer to stay put and then come out. Only a couple of seconds for Holden to hear the caller, too.

"Marshal Ryland?" the caller asked.

It was a man all right, but Holden had no idea if this was really Minton or not. Though Beatrice seemed to believe it was her husband.

"Where are you?" And that was just Holden's starter question. He had a boatload of others.

"In Silver Creek." Like Amanda, this guy sounded out of breath. "It's not safe here. Someone's trying to kill me."

"Who?" Holden snapped.

"I'm not sure. The person who hired someone to kidnap me. That's also the same person who's responsible for these babies being born."

Holden jumped right on that. "You know about the babies?"

"Yes." The caller paused. "I have one of them. A girl."

Holden certainly hadn't seen that coming. But

maybe he should have. Because if Beatrice had put this plan together, then the caller could be one of her hired guns. And this could be another attempt to get some ransom money or to draw them into the open.

"Start talking," Holden demanded. "Tell me why you have the baby and what you want."

"I only want her safe. I want to be safe, too."

"Then bring her here to the sheriff's office." Holden didn't figure the man would take him up on that.

And he didn't.

"I can't," the caller insisted. "Too risky."

"It was risky to break in to Amanda's hotel room, too," Holden growled.

"I was looking for something, anything I could find out about Conceptions Clinic, but I left as soon as I saw the car. The car with the baby. I took her, and now they're after us."

No way could Holden not react to that. The fear came, and it was bone-deep. That could be his niece out there, and he had to fight the kick of adrenaline to stop himself from going out there to look for her.

"Bring the baby here right now," Holden demanded.

But he was talking to himself because the man was no longer on the line.

"Lee?" Beatrice shouted, snatching back her phone so she could call him.

Holden ignored her for the moment and fired off a text to Josh, to warn him that there might be a baby nearby. And he waited.

Nicky was clearly having trouble tamping down her fears, too. Her gaze was firing all around as if she were looking for whatever she could do to keep the baby safe.

"It could have all been a lie," Holden reminded her. A reminder for himself, too.

However, Beatrice must have thought it was all real because she kept trying to get in touch with the caller again.

"What did he say to you before you brought me the phone?" Holden asked her.

Beatrice shook her head, and it took her a moment to answer. "Only that he was in danger and that he needed to talk to Marshal Holden Ryland."

So, the man had asked for him specifically. If it was indeed Minton, then that meant he knew a lot about this investigation. Was that why someone was after him? Had he figured out too much?

"He didn't ask about our son," Beatrice said under her breath, and then she started to cry.

"Go back to the interview room," Holden told

her again. "But leave your phone in case the man calls back."

"That man is my husband," she insisted. And she kept on insisting. Kept on crying, too.

Holden was about to repeat his order for her to move, but then he heard something he didn't want to hear. The door to the other interview room opened.

"What the hell is going on out here?" Oscar asked.

"My patience is at zero right now," Holden warned him. "Either you and your lawyer stay in the interview room with the door closed, or I'll put you both in a holding cell. Move!" Holden added when Oscar just stood there.

Oscar finally turned and went back into the room, but he'd barely gotten the door closed when there was another sound.

A gunshot.

The shot cracked through the air, and it was close. Too close.

That got Beatrice running away from the windows and to the interview room. What she didn't do was leave him her phone, and Holden didn't have time to remedy that now.

Because there was another shot.

Grayson hurried to the front of the building with Holden, and they both looked out. No sign of who'd fired those shots. Holden also kept an eye on Nicky and cursed when he saw that both her father and Beatrice were now at the back of the squad room, only a couple of feet from Nicky. Grayson didn't miss it, either.

"Go to Nicky," Grayson told him. "If I see the shooter, I'll let you know."

Holden debated what to do for a second. He didn't want to leave Grayson up front without backup, but he reminded himself that Nicky was the target here. Holden went to her, grabbing Beatrice's phone along the way. He maneuvered Nicky into the empty interview room, and he stood in the doorway.

"What can I do to help?" Nicky asked. She looked surprisingly strong for a woman who was so close to gunfire—yet again.

Holden passed Beatrice's phone to Nicky. "Try calling Minton again." It definitely wasn't just busywork, either, because if that man had been telling the truth, then he had the baby.

There was another shot. Then another. Both of them closer than the other shots had been. He hoped the deputies weren't in the middle of gunfire. The baby, too. If there was a baby.

"Minton or whoever that was isn't answering," Nicky informed him.

He was about to tell her to keep trying, but Holden's own phone buzzed. Since he didn't want to take his attention off Grayson and the front door, he handed his phone back to Nicky.

"It's Amanda," she said, and put the call on speaker.

"Who's shooting?" Amanda whispered.

"I was hoping you would know."

"No, I can't see any gunmen, but the shots sound close. Holden, I'm so scared."

"Where are you?" Holden asked.

"In the alley about three or four buildings from the sheriff's office. I'm hiding on the side of the Dumpster behind what looks to be a hardware store."

"Stay put. I can send a deputy to get you."

"No!" Amanda insisted. "I don't trust the deputies. I'm not even sure I can trust you."

"Then why even call me?" Holden cursed. "I'm trying to stop you from being killed."

At least he was if she was innocent, and since he didn't know if she was innocent or not, Holden wanted her alive so he could question her.

"I don't know what to do," Amanda sobbed. "I don't want to die. Oh, God. They're here. The gunmen are here."

Holden didn't get a chance to say anything to her because Amanda was no longer on the line. And worse, there was a series of shots. Six of them, and from the sound of it, they were being fired from different weapons.

"Amanda's in the back of the hardware store," Holden told Grayson.

This time it was Grayson who cursed. And Holden knew why. If the deputies were in a fight for their lives, a call or text might be a fatal distraction. Still, they had to do something if only to let the deputies know Amanda's location.

"Let Josh know about Amanda," Grayson finally said, but before Holden could even have Nicky start the text, Grayson's phone rang. "Hold off on that text. It's Josh."

Well, at least if Josh was calling that meant he was alive, but that didn't mean he or someone else hadn't been hurt.

As Nicky had done, Grayson put the call on speaker and placed his phone on the reception desk behind him. No doubt to free up his hands in case he had to return fire.

"I'm coming in," Josh immediately said. "And I'm not alone. Grayson, I found the baby."

EVEN THOUGH NICKY was several rooms away, she had no trouble hearing what Josh had just said.

There was a baby, and he had it.

That got Holden moving toward the front with Grayson, and both of them stood, shoulder-to-shoulder, their guns ready. At least there wasn't any gunfire at the moment, but time seemed to have stopped. Unlike the thoughts flying through her head. Those were speeding through her mind, and even though Nicky knew the worst could have happened, she prayed for the best.

For Josh and the baby's safety. For Kara's, too.

Although Holden warned her to stay back, Nicky still peered out from the doorway of the interview room, and she was able to see when Grayson and Holden stepped back. Making the way for Josh.

And he finally came in.

Josh had the baby clutched to his chest, but Nicky couldn't see much of the infant because she was wrapped in a blanket. Josh didn't stay near the door. He headed up the hall where Nicky was waiting.

"Where's Kara?" Grayson asked.

"Still looking for Minton and Amanda," Josh answered. "Kara and I got separated when the gunmen started shooting at us. Here, take her," he added, handing Nicky the baby. "I'll go back out and find Kara."

"I'll go," Grayson insisted, and he headed out.

Holden stayed near the front, probably to make sure those gunmen didn't show up, but he was volleying glances between Josh, the baby and her.

Nicky eased back the blanket, and the first thing she saw was the ginger hair. Identical to Carter's. And Annie's.

"This is Annie and Emmett's daughter," she told Holden when she managed to gather enough breath to speak. Of course, it would have to be verified with DNA, but Nicky was certain of it.

Certain, too, that the love she felt for the baby was instant. So was the fear. Because now they had to keep her safe. Soon, she'd need to deal with the shock she was feeling, too. She'd had to deal with a lot of things, including what was happening between Holden and her. But for now, she just held her niece and said a prayer of thanks.

However, Nicky wasn't very thankful when her father came rushing out of the interview room. She wanted to kick herself for blurting out that this was her niece because obviously her father had heard it.

Oscar didn't say anything. He just came closer, his attention fixed on the baby.

"Don't you dare mention a word about custody and court orders," Nicky warned him. "Because I've had more than enough of you and your threats."

She expected him to glare at her or toss out

one of his stinging remarks, but the shock must have taken over because he groaned and leaned against the wall.

"Is the baby okay?" Holden asked.

"She appears to be." The baby was squirming and fussing a little, but she didn't have any visible injuries, thank God. Along with the DNA test, though, she'd need to be checked by a doctor.

"How'd you get her?" Oscar asked Josh as Nicky continued to examine the baby.

"Luck," Josh answered. "When I was making my way through the alley to the hardware store, I saw her lying on the ground."

That sickened Nicky. Infuriated her, too. Because someone had been so careless with something so precious.

"I want to hold her," Oscar said.

Nicky shook her head. "Not until I'm sure you're innocent, and right now, I'm not sure of that at all."

Now she got the glare, and while it didn't please her, it didn't please Josh, either. "Come with me," Josh told her father. "You, too. Because I'm not any more convinced of your innocence than Nicky is."

"Where do you think you're taking us?" Oscar snapped.

"To a holding cell. It's for your own safety.

For ours, too, and please resist so I can handcuff you and charge you with some assorted crimes like interfering with an officer and impeding an investigation."

Oscar gave Josh a glare for that sarcasm. "This isn't over," her father warned her, but neither he nor his lawyer resisted when Josh led them out of the hall and to the other side of the building, where there were holding cells.

Nicky felt some relief at having Oscar away from the baby, but she knew he wouldn't stay away. It wouldn't be long at all before he got out of that cell and then came for this little girl as he'd been trying to do with Carter.

Josh was only gone a couple of minutes. Probably because he hadn't wanted to leave Nicky and the baby so close to yet another of their suspects—Beatrice.

"Tell me who did this," Nicky said to Josh. "Who put the baby there in that alley?"

Josh shook his head. "I don't know. When I found her, there was no one around. I didn't even get a good look at the gunmen."

The shooters were almost certainly from the same team of thugs who'd been tormenting them from the start, but that didn't explain why they would have left the baby like that. Or maybe they hadn't. Maybe Minton truly had managed to take her from them.

But then where was Minton?

"Let me trade places with Holden," Josh suggested. "And he can see his niece." He gave the baby another glance. "She looks like her mother."

She did. From all the photos Nicky had seen of Annie when she was a baby, this little girl was practically a genetic copy.

As soon as Josh was at the front door, Holden hurried back to her, and he gave the baby the same once-over that Nicky had. "I'll find out who did this. I promise."

She didn't doubt it. Didn't doubt the raw emotion he was feeling, either, because Nicky was experiencing the same thing. The problem was, they didn't have a lot of options for putting a stop to the dangerous situation they were in unless they found Amanda and Minton. There wasn't much she could do about Amanda now, but Minton was a different story.

Nicky tipped her head to the interview room and handed Holden back the phone he'd taken earlier from Beatrice. "Maybe Beatrice knows of another way we can try to reach her husband."

Holden didn't look any more optimistic about

that than she was, but he went into the room anyway. Beatrice was right there when he opened the door, and she'd clearly heard everything.

Considering all that had gone on, Nicky figured there'd be tears. Or at least some more concern than the woman had shown earlier. Or rather pretended to show.

"I've tried every way to contact my husband, and other than that call where I reached him earlier, I didn't talk to him," Beatrice insisted. "Obviously, he didn't want to get in touch with me before now, or he would have. And when he called, he didn't even want to speak to me. He wanted to talk to him." She flung her fingers in Holden's direction.

Still no tears, but Nicky heard the anger, and while she didn't want to speculate if it was real or not, Nicky could certainly understand why the wife of a missing man would feel that way. Unless Beatrice had had some part in her husband's disappearance, she might have thought he was dead.

This proved otherwise.

And it could also give Beatrice a complication she didn't want. If Minton had been dead, then their son would have likely inherited his estate, and that would have given Beatrice access to more money. That wouldn't happen, though, with Minton alive. Plus, now Beatrice couldn't play the part of the grieving widow.

"Lee's probably been with her this whole time," Beatrice snarled.

Her. As in Minton's mistress. Sharon Bachman. During interviews with the police, Sharon had admitted to the affair but had claimed she had no idea where Minton was.

"Call *her*," Holden insisted.

Nicky wasn't sure Beatrice would do that, but if the woman had refused, Nicky could have managed to contact Sharon. But having Beatrice do it would save time because Nicky was betting that Beatrice knew the woman's number.

She did.

Beatrice had the number in her recent calls, and she pressed it. When Holden prompted Beatrice to put it on speaker, she did. Though judging from the way her mouth tightened, she wasn't looking forward to any part of this call.

"Have you heard from Lee?" Sharon asked the moment she answered, and Nicky heard something in the woman's voice that she hadn't heard in Beatrice's—genuine concern.

Beatrice didn't answer, and she looked at Holden as if waiting for him to tell her what to say. However, he didn't tell her. He took the phone from her.

"Sharon, I'm Marshal Holden Ryland, and a man claiming to be Senator Minton called me about twenty minutes ago. Has Minton been in touch with you?"

"No. He called you? Is he okay? Where is he?" Her words rushed out, filled with sobs, relief and more worry.

"I'm not positive it was actually Minton—"

"It was Lee," Beatrice interrupted, and she went closer to the phone. "Sharon, if you know where Lee is, for God's sake, tell us."

"I don't know, but he's alive, right? Did he say what had happened to him?"

"You'd know that better than we would," Beatrice growled. "Because I suspect he's been with you since you're his flavor of the month. What, did you two have a lovers' spat and he left when he realized what a bimbo you really are?"

"No! Of course not. I swear, I haven't spoken to him or seen him since he went missing."

Beatrice made a sound to indicate she wasn't buying that. "Is Lee pretending to be in danger because he's trying to save face?"

"What are you talking about?" Sharon asked, and Nicky wanted to know the same thing.

"I think you convinced Lee to run off with you, and then when he figured out what he was giving up by being with you—his career and his reputation—he broke things off and pretended that he'd been kidnapped or something. But now he's been taken for real."

"Oh, God." Sharon gave another sob. "You know for certain that Lee's really been kidnapped?"

Nicky and Holden exchanged glances, and she could tell from the look in Holden's eyes that he didn't believe they were going to get anything from Sharon. The woman didn't seem to have a clue what'd happened to Minton.

"If Minton contacts you, tell him to call me," Holden instructed Sharon.

"I will, and please do the same for me. I have to know if he's all right."

Holden assured her that he would, and he ended the call. Perfect timing because Beatrice appeared to be gearing up to sling another round of insults.

"Am I free to go?" Beatrice asked.

"Aren't you even going to look at the baby to see if she might be yours?" Holden asked.

Beatrice's mouth tightened. "I heard Nicky say it was Emmett and Annie's baby."

"Yeah, but you haven't taken our word for anything else," Holden said. "Why would you on something as important as this?"

"I don't like your tone," Beatrice snapped. "I

don't know anything more about these babies than you do." However, she did spare the baby a glance. "And I agree that she is Emmett and Annie's. She doesn't look anything like me, my son or Lee."

"And yet the kidnappers contacted you for ransom money," Holden persisted.

"Because they were trying to scam me."

"But the scam would be on your husband, not you, since the money is his."

If Beatrice's eyes narrowed any further, she wouldn't have been able to see. "I'm leaving."

"Gunmen and kidnappers are still out there," Nicky reminded her.

"I'd rather be with them than stay another minute here with you," Beatrice snarled, and she headed for the door.

"Should I stop her?" Josh asked Holden.

Holden shook his head. "Let her go," he answered, but then stopped when they saw the man who was coming in through the front of the building.

Not one of their suspects or one of the gunmen, but it was someone who put Nicky's heart right back in her throat.

Drury.

She hadn't seen him since the attack that could have killed him. The attack she was partly responsible for, but Drury, like some of the other Rylands, might think she was entirely to blame.

Nicky certainly felt that way now.

He was the same height as Holden and had a similar build. Of course, both were good-looking. All the Ryland men were. But unlike Holden, Drury had a dangerous edge to him, and he always seemed to scowl. At least he did whenever he was around her. But then, she had earned each and every one of his scowls and much more.

"Can I help?" Drury asked Holden. He didn't come closer, though his attention landed on the baby.

"This isn't Annie and Emmett's son," Holden explained. "It's their daughter. They had twins."

Drury didn't react to that, but he spared Nicky a glance while he walked toward them. He nodded once he saw the newborn girl. "Yeah" was all he said for several long moments. "I'm on the team that's going through the files at Conceptions Clinic, but we haven't found anything useful."

Nicky hadn't known he was part of that investigation, but it didn't surprise her since Drury was an FBI agent. A good one, too, and she was thankful he was part of the team. Drury wouldn't give up until he'd exhausted every possible bit of information.

"I was about to take Nicky and the baby out of here," Holden volunteered.

Maybe it was the way Holden said her name, but it caused Drury to look at her again. Holden's tone hadn't exactly been a loving one, but it didn't have its usual venom, either.

"Are you two back together?" Drury asked. A muscle flickered in his jaw, though she wasn't sure how any muscles could stir there because his expression was rock-hard.

"No," Nicky answered at the same moment Holden said, "It's complicated."

Drury shifted his attention back to his brother. "It always is." He gave Holden a pat on the arm, and using just his index finger, Drury eased back the blanket to have a better look at the baby. "I don't want the past to get in the way of making sure the baby's all right. Her twin brother, too."

"Thanks for that," Holden answered, and Nicky silently added her own thanks. It wasn't exactly a truce, but she would take it.

"You need an escort to wherever you're going?" Drury asked.

Holden nodded. "Can you follow us and make sure we're not ambushed along the way?"

"Of course." Drury turned back toward the door, but he'd hardly made it a step when the sound of Holden's phone stopped them.

Nicky glanced at the screen and saw Grayson's name there.

"Any sign of Amanda or Minton?" Holden asked the moment he answered.

"No. I'm at the Dumpster where Amanda said she was. She's not here, but we found something." Grayson cursed. "Blood."

Chapter Fourteen

Holden looked down at his niece as he held her. At that precious little face. And he felt the same emotions that he'd felt when he held Carter. He loved her, would do whatever it took to protect her, but he also knew she was in danger.

Nicky, too.

Holden's phone dinged, and he saw the text message from Drury on the screen. His brother had made it back to San Antonio and was at Conceptions Clinic—where Holden hoped like the devil there was still something to find that would help put an end to the danger.

"Everything okay?" Nicky asked.

He nodded. Everything was okay with Drury anyway. They hadn't managed to catch the kidnappers, and that meant the threat was still there, and it left Holden with no choice but to send the baby to the safe house as well. Especially now that they might not have Amanda to give them answers.

Because Amanda might be dead.

There hadn't been a large amount of blood found by the Dumpster, but it was enough to cause concern. He was also concerned that it had been hours since the latest attack, and no one had heard from her. Ditto for Minton. With no other new information in the investigation, Holden was worried they were stalled.

Well, no other new info than the baby.

The newborn girl was definitely news. Amanda hadn't said anything about delivering twins, but Holden remembered her mentioning something at the hospital about being put to sleep during the C-section. If that was true, then it was possible she hadn't even known.

"Wouldn't a woman have realized she was carrying twins?" Holden looked up at Nicky with that question. She was in the process of warming up another bottle of formula—something they'd both mastered, what with the practice they'd gotten with Carter and now his sister.

She shrugged. "You'd think so, but maybe the person responsible didn't allow Amanda to see the ultrasounds. Besides, even if Amanda did suspect it, she might have been too afraid to say anything."

Yeah, because if Amanda had started asking a lot of questions, it would have put her in danger. If she'd realized something was wrong with the whole surrogate plan, then she might have decided just to stay quiet.

But Holden shook his head. "She's still a suspect, though."

"I agree," Nicky said without hesitation. "She could have put the blood there to throw suspicion off her. And of our three suspects, she was still in the best position at Conceptions to have orchestrated all of this."

True. Except for the part about Amanda being fired, but then she could have arranged for that as well, just so it would look as if she was no longer connected to Conceptions.

"What about Minton?" she asked. "You think either Sharon or he have anything to do with what's going on?"

It was something Holden had already considered. And dismissed. "The last thing Sharon probably wants is for Beatrice and Minton to have a child."

"I agree, and there are some problems with Beatrice's theory of Sharon and Minton running off. If that'd happened and Minton had indeed changed his mind, he could have just shown up at a police station with a story about being kidnapped. I doubt he would have involved himself in the mess at Conceptions."

No, but it made Holden go back to one of the questions he couldn't answer. How had Minton gotten his hands on Emmett and Annie's baby? If he got a chance to talk to the man again, that was something Holden definitely wanted to know.

Nicky returned with the bottle and handed it to him. Unlike Carter, the little girl latched on and kept drinking. Not for just a couple of sips, either.

"Bittersweet, isn't it?" Nicky asked when she saw him staring at the little girl.

Yeah, it was. "Annie and Emmett wanted a baby so much, and now they have two. Twins. And they aren't even here to see them." That caused a pain so deep within Holden that it felt as if the pain had seeped into his bones.

Now, the pain would be even deeper because after just meeting her, Holden was going to have to say goodbye. And soon. Josh and another deputy were already on their way to pick up the baby and drive her to the safe house with Carter, Landon and the others. It was the right thing to do, their only option really, but that didn't make it any easier.

"What will happen to them?" Nicky asked. She touched her fingertips to the baby's toes, which were peeking out from the bottom of her pink gown.

Holden knew she wasn't just talking about the immediate future. "I think we've neutralized Oscar for now what with him being on the surveillance footage at the ransom drop."

"Yes." Nicky paused, repeated that. "But I'm sure he was furious at being placed in a holding cell."

Holden was certain of it, but Nicky and he hadn't waited around to find out. As soon as Grayson and the other deputies had returned to the sheriff's office, Holden and Kara had brought Nicky and the baby back to Kayla's house.

"My father will keep trying to get custody," Nicky continued after Holden had finished feeding the baby and had put her against his shoulder to attempt a burp. "That's why I think we should make our own petition to get at least temporary guardianship of them. A joint petition," she added. "We could share custody."

Their gazes connected. "Under the same roof?" he asked.

But it wasn't just a simple question of logistics. The memory of their kiss in the ER was still fresh. Heck, it'd be fresh months from now because he'd probably still be feeling it.

Nicky felt it, too.

The corner of her mouth lifted. "Would it matter if we were under separate roofs?"

Not in the least. The heat would still be there, but this was the exact opposite of out of sight, out of mind. Being next to each other would lead to things Holden wasn't sure he, or his family, could accept.

He didn't answer. Didn't have time because he heard Kara open the front door. It didn't take long for Holden to hear voices, too. Josh and Mason. Several moments later, his cousins came into the kitchen.

"How's she doing?" Josh asked, going straight to the baby.

"Good. Thanks again for finding her," Holden answered, and he refused to think of what would have happened to her if Josh hadn't been in the right place at the right time.

"A girl," Mason remarked, moving closer as well. Since this was Mason, he didn't seem to have an opinion if that was a good thing, but as Nicky had done earlier, he touched the baby's toes.

"Don't get all sentimental on us," Josh joked.

"Not sentimental," Mason growled. Of course, every time he spoke, it sounded like a growl. "Girls are just easier to diaper than boys. Does she have a name yet?"

That started some surprised looks, and Mason huffed. "You should come up with something soon before she gets a nickname like Scarlett or Strawberry."

Yeah, Holden definitely didn't want the kid getting stuck with that.

"We could call her Kate," Nicky suggested. "It was Annie's middle name, after our grandmother."

That caused Josh and Mason to nod in approval. Holden approved, too, and it worked since Carter was Emmett's middle name. But for some reason, with the baby having a name, it made all of this even harder. Because it was yet another reminder that this baby—Kate Ryland—was part of the family. Part of him, too.

Holden hadn't needed to think of how high the stakes were, but that did it.

Josh took the baby, holding her so that Holden and Nicky could get a goodbye kiss. "We'll call you as soon as we've made it to the safe house," Josh assured them.

Nicky and Holden thanked him, and after Mason scooped up the diaper bag with the baby supplies, they all went to the door. Mainly because Mason didn't waste any time getting out of the house, there was no long goodbye. Which was probably a good thing. However, Nicky and Holden stood in the door and watched until they drove away.

With Kate.

It felt as if someone had put a fist around his heart and was squeezing pretty damn hard.

"I need a drink," Holden grumbled. Heck, he needed six of them, but would settle for just one so he could keep a clear head.

He reset the security system, and Kara headed back to the office, where she'd been monitoring the cameras and sensors positioned around the property. Holden would relieve her soon, but for now he went in search of that much-needed drink. He found one in the bar in the family room, and he made a mental note to thank Kayla for stocking the good stuff.

Holden poured himself a glass of whiskey and lifted the bottle to offer Nicky one as well, but she shook her head. That's when he saw that she was blinking back tears.

Hell.

He should have known this was going to send her crashing. It wasn't just the baby, either, but Nicky had to be dealing with the aftermath of being shot. The aftermath, too, of knowing this nightmare was far from being over.

Holden downed the drink and went to her, ready to pull her into his arms. It would be a mistake, of course. They were under the same roof. Semi-alone. And no one was currently shooting at them.

A perfect storm.

But he could try to keep it at just a comforting hug.

Nicky didn't play by the rules, though, and it was obvious she'd need much more than just a hug from him. The moment he reached for her, she reached for him. And she was the one who started the kiss.

NICKY HADN'T KNOWN exactly what she was going to do when Holden had started toward her, but she heard him say something under his breath.

A perfect storm.

Yes, that's exactly what this was.

But it was a storm that she had no intention of stopping. She didn't care about the consequences. Not at the moment anyway. She would later, but there were plenty of other things she would have to deal with later.

"Your arm," Holden said like a warning.

That wouldn't stop her, either. The only thing that would put an end to this was Holden telling her that it wasn't going to happen. But he wasn't saying anything like that. In fact, he'd stopped talking and was kissing her.

Exactly what Nicky wanted him to do.

He tasted of whiskey, but there was also Holden's own familiar taste beneath that. She hadn't needed that taste to start the fire simmering inside her. The fire was always there whenever she was around Holden. But it only added to the moment, and this was a moment she intended to savor.

Because she might not have Holden like this again.

Yes, later she'd have to deal with a lot of things, including the fact that they might never be able to get past their old wounds and do something more than just have sex with each other. For now, though, this was enough.

Holden made the most of that *enough*. He deepened the kiss, and he slipped his arm around her waist, bringing her closer to him. He was gentle. Too gentle. A reminder that he was thinking about the stitches on her arm. Part of Nicky appreciated that, but she needed more from him now.

She dropped her hand to his chest, opening the buttons, and slid her fingers over his chest. She got just the reaction she wanted. He made a sound of pleasure, and the kiss kicked up a notch. So did her heartbeat.

So did the heat.

He turned her, putting her back against the bar, anchoring her in place. Nicky immediately felt the pressure of his body on hers, and it settled her for a moment. Just long enough to allow her to savor the feeling, but it wasn't long before it only made her want more.

Holden gave her more.

He pushed up her top, lowered his head and kissed the tops of her breasts. Then, he pushed down the cups of her bra and took her into his mouth.

Now, it was Nicky's turn to make a sound of pleasure, and her legs would have buckled if Holden hadn't kept her in place against the bar. She made even more of those sounds when he added some touching to those kisses. She wanted to think he knew just the right spot to make her burn because they'd been together before, but the truth was, he'd known all the right spots their first time.

And he repeated that now and upped the ante by going lower and kissing her stomach.

Nicky was wearing loose jeans that she'd borrowed from Kayla's closet, and Holden unzipped them. He didn't stop kissing, either, and it became very clear what he had in mind. Some foreplay that she was sure would set the fire inside her blazing. But there was a problem.

"Kara could come in," she said breathlessly.

Holden still didn't stop, but he did curse. And he shoved down her jeans just enough to deliver one melting kiss to the exact place she wanted his lips to touch.

If Kara came in now, she'd certainly get an eyeful, and Holden must have accepted that because he scooped her up in his arms. She didn't know where he was taking her, didn't care because he continued to kiss her with every step.

They didn't go far. To one of the guest rooms just a few rooms away. Holden shut the door and locked it before he carried her to the bed. He didn't join her, though, and Nicky reached for him, to pull him down to her. But she stopped.

Because he stripped off his shirt.

And she lost her breath in the process.

He was perfect, just as she remembered him. His body was chiseled—not from working out in a gym but from working on the ranch. Toned and tanned. Yes, perfect.

It got even better.

He unzipped his jeans, and the rest of his clothes came off.

Nicky was well aware she was staring. Couldn't stop herself. Mercy, how could she feel this way just by looking at him? She didn't have time to figure that out, though, because he finally got on the bed with her.

"Let's do something about getting you naked, too," he drawled.

She would have gladly helped him with that if he hadn't made her senseless with another of those scalding kisses. But thankfully Holden had no trouble peeling off her top and bra. Had no trouble kissing her breasts again and driving her crazy.

He started the trail of kisses again, retracing his steps to her stomach. Her zipper was already undone so he shimmied the jeans off her, removing her panties with them.

And now she got that kiss she'd been wanting.

Nicky could have sworn the earth tipped on its axis. Maybe it did. Holden was certainly working some magic, and Nicky knew this would end much too soon if it continued.

She latched onto him, dragging him back up toward her, but he seemed to have his own notion about that as well. He dug through his jeans and located a condom in his wallet.

Something that made her groan.

Here she'd gotten so caught up that she hadn't remembered that they needed to use protection. At least one of them was thinking straight.

When Holden returned to the bed, he maneuvered them to the headboard and adjusted their positions until they were in a sitting position with her on his lap.

"Your arm," he said.

Nicky still hadn't managed the thinking-straight part so it took her a moment to realize this way there wouldn't be any pressure on her stitches. Yes, Holden was definitely thinking a lot straighter than she was.

So she did something about that.

She reached between their bodies, helped him with the condom and then took him inside her. Deep and quick. While she kissed him. After a few strokes, she thought maybe she'd managed to cloud his mind as well.

There was a problem with that, though. This was still all going to end too soon, and there was nothing she could do to stop that. The need was too great. The fire, too hot.

Holden must have realized that because he caught her hips and began controlling the rhythm, bringing her toward the only thing Nicky wanted now.

For him to take her over the edge. For him to ease the fire and the storm that was raging out of control.

And that's what he did.

Holden pushed into her and sent her flying. The climax slammed through her. Nicky couldn't speak. Couldn't breathe. But she could feel. And what she felt was Holden falling over the edge with her.

HOLDEN GAVE HIMSELF a couple of seconds to catch his breath. Then another couple of seconds to come to his senses, and he checked to make sure Nicky wasn't in pain, or that her stitches weren't torn.

She was clearly okay.

Nicky's face was right against his, and she was so relaxed that the muscles in her body had gone slack. There was no indication whatsoever that she was hurting. Not from her injury anyway. But when she lifted her head, and her gaze met his, Holden did see something he wasn't sure he liked.

"Don't regret this," she whispered.

Too late. He already did.

Not because it wasn't mind-blowing sex. It had been. But because he was in bed with someone in his protective custody, and he'd just completely lost focus. Definitely not something that would help them. Plus, there was another complication. One that he didn't especially want to consider, but it came to the forefront of his mind anyway.

Maybe this had been more than just mind-blowing sex.

"You are regretting it," she said. Nicky huffed and moved off him.

That was Holden's cue to move, too, and he eased off the bed and went into the bathroom. Despite the realization that this had just complicated the heck out of things, Holden was already thinking about being with her again.

Soon.

And with that on his mind, he came back into

the bedroom and saw that Nicky and he were not on the same page when it came to sex. She was already out of the bed and getting dressed.

"Are *you* regretting what happened?" he asked. And he hated that it felt like a punch to the gut that she might be.

She didn't look at him when she pulled on her jeans. "Not the way you're thinking." She put on her shoes and would have headed for the door if Holden hadn't stepped in front of her to stop her.

Holden tried to figure out what was going on in her head but couldn't tell. She seemed angry or something, and he glanced at her arm again to make sure that wasn't the problem.

"I'm not in pain," she insisted. "I just want to get back to work. I have Paul's files to go through."

Since she obviously wasn't in the mood to talk about what just happened, Holden leaned in and kissed her. Judging from the slight sound of surprise she made, Nicky definitely hadn't been expecting that. Heck, he hadn't been expecting it, either, but whenever he was around Nicky, he always seemed to be flying by the seat of his pants.

Holden kissed her until that sound of surprise turned to one of pleasure, and she sort of melted into his arms. Considering he was still naked and that his body was revved up into overdrive, it felt better than good.

And that was the problem.

Holden understood why she was in flight mode, or at least why she'd been just seconds earlier.

"I'm scared, too," he admitted, and he wasn't talking about the danger now.

She nodded. "I just don't want my heart crushed again."

Again?

He nearly asked if he'd been the one to cause a heart crushing, but Holden knew that he had been. They hadn't exactly been in a relationship before, but it had certainly been the start of one, and it had all come crashing down when Drury had nearly been killed.

She looked down between them. At his naked body. "You're very tempting," she said, causing him to smile.

He looked at her mouth. "Tempting," Holden repeated.

Nicky smiled, too, and that moment washed away some of the regret, some of the doubts about that possible heart crushing. But it didn't last. That's because his phone buzzed. Holden fished it from his jeans pocket, and they both saw whose name popped up on the screen.

Kara.

Considering the deputy was just up the hall, or at least that's where she was supposed to be, this probably wasn't good news.

"Holden, are you in there?" Kara asked the moment he answered and put the call on speaker.

"I'm here." That sent him scrambling for his clothes.

"You need to come right away and take a look at the computer that monitors the security," she said. "We have an intruder on the grounds."

Chapter Fifteen

Nicky's heart jumped to her throat, and just like that, the heat between she and Holden was gone. Oh, God. Had the kidnappers found them?

"I'll be right there," Holden assured Kara, and he hurriedly dressed.

Nicky made sure her clothes were fixed, too, and then followed him up the hall. Kara was in an office. Not an ordinary office, though. There were no windows in the room, and it was jammed with equipment. Six monitors, all with split screens to show every angle of the grounds. But it was dark outside, and it took Nicky a moment to look at each one.

Nicky finally saw the man near one of the fences.

There wasn't much of a moon, but the camera was rigged like night-vision goggles. Without that, he would have just blended into the darkness, which was probably what he'd intended.

But with the night vision, he looked a little like a ghost.

"Are there security lights out there?" Nicky asked.

Holden shook his head. "But there are plenty if he gets closer to the house. Those are motion-activated."

Good. So, if anyone tried to get near the place to start shooting, they should trigger the lights. The alarm, too.

"He doesn't appear to be armed," Kara said, "but then he's staying in the shadows so it's hard to tell."

In this case the shadows were from a cluster of towering pecan trees and the night itself, and while the man might not have been armed, he was definitely hiding between the trees.

"Try to zoom in on his face," Holden instructed.

This particular one didn't have on a ski mask, but there were too many shadows for them to clearly see his face. Which was probably also part of his plan. After all, if he'd trespassed onto private property, then he was probably up to no good.

Nicky glanced at the other monitors but didn't see anyone else. Thank goodness. That didn't mean they weren't in danger, but at least they weren't facing down an entire army of kidnappers. Not yet anyway. It could be this guy was sent to scope things out, maybe even to test the security system.

But how had he found them?

"Has Kayla had trouble in the past with people trespassing?" Nicky asked because she had to consider that this person may not even be connected to the attacks.

Kara shook her head. "None that I know of. Everyone in the area knows she has a state-of-the-art security system."

So, the man was likely there because of them. Not exactly a thought to help settle her nerves.

Nicky had her attention so focused on the monitor that she gasped when the sound shot through the room. Not the threat that her body had anticipated. But rather Holden's phone buzzed.

"Minton," he said, looking at the screen. Holden put this call on speaker, too.

"Can you see me?" Minton asked.

At that moment the man leaned out from the tree, and Nicky got a better look at his face. Yes, it was Senator Minton all right, but he quickly ducked behind the tree.

Holden didn't jump to answer, probably because he didn't want to confirm that they were indeed on the property and watching.

"I put a tracking device on your car," Minton added. "That's how I knew where you were."

"A tracking device?" Holden challenged. "How did you manage to get one of those when you were on the run?"

"It was in the baby's blanket. When I realized what it was, I left the baby in the alley and sneaked into the parking lot. I knew which car was yours because I saw you drive up in it."

Holden cursed, and Nicky hated that he would blame himself for this, but there'd been a lot of craziness going on in Silver Creek, and they hadn't exactly been focusing on the car. She prayed that didn't turn out to be a fatal mistake.

"You left a baby in the alley," Holden snarled. "Tell me why the hell you would do that, especially considering there was gunfire."

"I didn't want to take her out into the open, and I knew those kidnappers weren't going to do anything to harm her."

"And how did you know that?" Nicky blurted out. She couldn't help herself. The anger hit her hard, and she wanted to throttle this fool for doing that to a baby. "They could have hurt her or worse."

"No," Minton argued. "I heard them call her their two-million-dollar baby, and I knew they wouldn't risk hurting her. They were shooting at the deputies."

"And at you?" Holden challenged.

"No," the man repeated. "Those men were never after me." He paused. "Is the baby all right? And my son—is he okay?"

"The baby girl is fine. I'm not sure about your son, though. I haven't seen him." Holden's voice was filled with just as much anger as Nicky's. "Now, tell me how you got the newborn girl?"

"Some men had her in a car just up the street from the sheriff's office. I was hiding, watching them, because I thought maybe they were the same men who'd kidnapped me. But they weren't."

The anger was still there, but Nicky felt something else—surprise.

"You're sure?" she asked.

"Positive. My kidnappers have held me for two weeks, and even though they wore masks, I know how they moved, and the sounds of their voices. The ones who had the baby wore ski masks, too, and they were on their phones a lot. Whoever they were talking to told them to put a tracking device on your car. They left the baby alone, I took her. That's when I saw that she had a tracking device in her blanket."

Mercy. Nicky looked at Holden, and he shook his head, maybe telling her not to borrow trouble. But Nicky was already thinking the worst.

Had those kidnappers put a tracking device on Nicky's car, too?

She frantically searched the screens and didn't see anyone, but there were a lot of barns, two guesthouses and several other outbuildings. Maybe those kidnappers had managed to get past security and were already on the grounds.

"I'm glad the baby's safe," Minton continued several moments later, "but that's not why I'm calling. I need your help, and I'm not sure I can trust anyone else."

"And why would you trust me?" Holden snapped.

"Because of Nicky. She's been trying to find me."

"So has half the state," Holden quickly pointed out.

"Maybe, but I heard one of the kidnappers talking to a cop once. Or maybe the guy was an ex-cop. I could tell he had some kind of law enforcement background from the slang he used."

"Or maybe he just watched a lot of crime shows." Holden kept his attention on Minton. The man hadn't moved an inch. "How did you get away from the kidnappers?"

"I offered one of them money. Lots of it. Not to the one who was talking with the cop, but the other one. He helped me escape, but something went wrong. Other kidnappers came after us. They killed him and tried to kill me. That's why I need your help. I want you to assure me that my son and I will be protected."

Holden stayed quiet a moment. "Who hired those kidnappers who took you, and are they connected to what happened at Conceptions?"

"Conceptions," Minton repeated like a profanity. "Yes, they're connected. Or at least I think they are. My kidnappers knew about my son, but they didn't take credit for what went on. In fact, the one who didn't end up helping me said it was a scam he wished he'd thought of."

A scam. Nicky hadn't needed anything else to anger her, but that did it. "Who's behind this *scam*?" she demanded.

"My wife. At least maybe she is. Or maybe she only had part in kidnapping me."

Holden jumped right on it. "Why would you say that?"

"Because my kidnappers never demanded a ransom. They just held me captive, and I had a lot of time to think about why they would do that. I think it was to give Beatrice some time to rob me blind."

That was one of Nicky's theories, too, but that didn't mean she was dismissing Beatrice's involvement at Conceptions. The baby—the Minton heir—was the perfect way to hang on to some of her husband's money.

"If you think your wife is guilty," Holden went on, "then why did you break in to Amanda's room at the hotel?"

"I was looking for something, anything to tie her to the Conceptions babies. She was a businesswoman, and I thought it was suspicious that she would become a surrogate. Especially a surrogate for a shady operation like the one going on at Conceptions." Minton huffed. "Will you help me now?"

Nicky saw the debate in Holden's eyes. Yes, he could call the sheriff's office, but he could be leading them into an ambush if those kidnappers were nearby. The goons could have put Minton up to this and could be hidden nearby with a gun pointed at him.

"Go back over the fence and toward the road," Holden finally said, "and I'll have some of my cousins come and get you."

"That's not safe," Minton argued. "I need to stay hidden or else they'll find me."

Holden didn't have time to respond though because there was a sound. A series of soft beeps. It took Nicky a moment to pick through all the screens and see what had caused those beeps.

A dark blue SUV.

It was coming up the road directly toward

the house, and the closer it got to the house, the more security lights flared on.

"Are you expecting anyone?" Kara asked.

"No," Holden answered.

And he drew his gun.

FROM THE MOMENT Holden had seen Minton on the monitor, he'd known this was going to be trouble. He just hadn't expected trouble to come so soon.

"Should I call the sheriff?" Kara asked.

Holden knew that Grayson and the others were neck-deep in this investigation, and this could still turn out to be nothing. But Holden figured that was wishful thinking on his part. Best to go ahead and alert Grayson, especially since it would take backup a while to get there.

"Call him," Holden answered, "but tell him about Minton. Minton might have tampered with the sensors on the back fence."

Or else Minton could have been forced to tamper with them. Holden still wasn't convinced that the senator was alone, and the kidnappers could have put him up to this. There were still questions to which they didn't have an answer, though.

Who was controlling the kidnappers?

"What can I do to help?" Nicky asked as Kara made the call to Grayson.

His first instinct was to tell her to hide, and he still might do that, but for now Holden opened the storage cabinet and took out a gun that Landon had told him would be there. In fact, there wasn't just one gun but three. Holden only hoped he didn't need them and that what he was doing was overkill.

"Keep watching the monitors," he told Kara. "I'm going to the front of the house to see if I can get a better look at our visitors. There's an intercom by the front door so you can talk to me through that." It would free up his hands if he didn't have to hold his phone.

"Should I go with you?" Nicky asked.

"Not a chance. Wait here." But he had to add something else. Something she wouldn't want to hear. "If anything goes wrong, I need you to stay in here and get down, understand?" he asked.

Holden waited until she nodded before he brushed a kiss on her mouth and hurried to the foyer. There were stained glass windows on each side of the door, and he looked out just as the SUV was coming to a stop in the circular drive.

There were no other vehicles visible on the grounds because Holden had parked in the garage. There were some lights on in the house but none that their visitors would be able to see from the front.

Holden waited. Watching for any movement inside the SUV, but it was hard to tell who or how many were inside because of the heavily tinted windows.

He pressed the intercom button. "Kara, can you zoom in on the SUV?" And he immediately heard the clicks on the computer keyboard Kara was using.

"I've zoomed in as much as I can, but the windows are too dark."

"Try getting a different angle from one of the other cameras," he instructed. "Nicky, you keep an eye on Minton."

Holden moved away from the intercom but left it on so he'd still be able to hear Nicky and Kara. He, too, tried a different angle. He went to the window in the living room and peered around the edge. The security lights hit the windshield just right so that Holden could see the silhouette of someone inside.

Or rather two silhouettes.

A driver and someone in the front passenger seat.

That didn't mean, however, that there were only two of them because if these were the hired thugs, there could be more in the backseat.

"Minton's on the move," Nicky blurted out.

Hell. Holden didn't need this now. "Is he coming toward the house?"

"Not at the moment. He's skirting along the fence line, though. There's a barn about an eighth of a mile from where he is, and he could be trying to get to it." Nicky paused. "He looks scared, and he keeps glancing over his shoulder."

Holden didn't like the sound of that at all. Of course, there wasn't much he liked about any of this. The only silver lining was that the babies were tucked away at the safe house.

He hoped.

The knot in his stomach tightened, and even though he knew this wouldn't help steady Nicky, it needed to be done.

"Don't take your eyes off Minton," Holden told her. "But call Landon and make sure everything's okay."

He had no trouble hearing Nicky suck in a hard breath. Practically a gasp. Something he totally understood. It cut him to the core that their attackers might have found a way to get to Landon and the babies, too.

The moments crawled by. Not his heartbeat, though. It was racing now and so was his breath. Still, all Holden could do was wait and listen as Nicky called Landon and filled him in on what was happening.

"They're all okay," Nicky finally said. "Landon says to keep him posted."

Holden would, if he could. "Where's Minton right now?"

"Still skulking toward the barn. Still looking around as if someone's going to jump out at him. He's getting close enough to the barn, though, that he'll trigger the security lights. If someone really is tracking him, that'll make it much easier for them."

Yeah, but there wasn't much Holden could do about that now. If and when Minton made it closer to the house, he'd deal with it then. But since the barn doors were wide-open, Minton would be able to run inside even if the lights gave away his location.

"Uh, Holden?" Kara said. "We have a problem. All the monitors just went blank. All I'm getting is static."

It felt as if someone had grabbed hold of his throat. No. This couldn't be happening.

"Try to reboot the system," Holden instructed.

More seconds crawled by.

"It's not working," Kara said. "Somebody's jammed the whole system."

Yeah, definitely wasn't what he wanted to hear. But then something else got Holden's attention. He saw the passenger door of the SUV open.

Then he saw the gun.

Except it wasn't a gun. It was some kind of launcher, and whoever was holding it had it aimed directly at the house.

Chapter Sixteen

Nicky kept watch at the door of the office as Kara tried once again to reboot the security system. She didn't want to think the worst—that someone had tampered with it and was ready to attack—but it was hard not to think just that what with everything that'd gone on.

"I believe someone's using a jamming device," Kara said. "I'm going to call the security company and see if they can access the cameras a different way."

Kara was taking out her phone when they heard the footsteps. Someone was running toward them.

"Get down!" Holden shouted.

Nicky didn't have time to even move before she heard the sound of shattering glass. Then, an even louder sound.

A blast.

It seemed to shake the entire house, and it

caused the fear to slam into her. *Holden*. God, had he been hurt?

She leaned out into the hall and saw him running toward them. Not hurt, thank goodness, but Nicky wasn't sure it would stay that way.

Because there was a second explosion.

"They're using grenades," Holden said when he reached them. "We're going to have to move."

He didn't wait for Nicky to do that. Holden hooked his arm around her waist, and with Kara right behind them, they hurried toward the back of the house. Not a second too soon, either.

The third blast was even louder than the others, and Nicky heard the sound of walls and maybe even the roof collapsing. Their attackers were literally trying to bring down the house with them inside it.

"Stay away from the windows," Holden reminded them when they reached the kitchen.

Hard to do that, though, since there were three large windows that faced the backyard. That's probably why Holden led them into the massive pantry.

The lights weren't on, and Holden kept it that way. No doubt so that those thugs wouldn't be able to pinpoint their exact location. However, whoever was shooting those grenades had to know that they would try to escape, and that they'd likely do that through the back so they could get as far away as possible from the explosions—and their attackers.

The fourth blast was even louder than the others, and with this one, Nicky smelled something that caused her heart to slam against her ribs.

Smoke.

Holden cursed, and Nicky knew why. It would take more grenades to destroy the house, and it was such a big place that they could probably find a safe area to hide until backup arrived. But if there was smoke, there was also likely fire, and that meant they'd have to get out.

"Stay here," Holden instructed, and he hurried to the exact place he'd told them to avoid.

The windows.

He looked out the side of the one nearest to them, but he also kept watch behind him, too. That's when Nicky knew she had to do something to help. She didn't know if it was possible for their attackers to get to them through the front of the house, but it was too big of a chance to take. She stepped out just enough so she could better keep watch. Kara did the same.

"I don't see Minton," Holden said after looking out the back.

That didn't mean he wasn't there. Nicky doubted the senator would have kept running toward the front of the house once he heard the explosion. Of course, he could be anywhere now that the sensors were off. It was the same for their attackers. They could already be in the back, waiting for them.

That gave her a new slam of adrenaline that she didn't need.

The smoke kept coming at them. Thick, dark and suffocating. They definitely wouldn't be able to stay here much longer.

Holden looked back, meeting Nicky's gaze, and she could see the apology in his expression. He was silently saying he was sorry for letting things get to this point. Of course, he would put all of this on his shoulders and would see it as a failure on his part. It wasn't. Whoever wanted her dead just wasn't stopping, and now Kara and Holden had gotten caught in the cross fire.

"This way," Holden ordered.

He didn't lead them out the back door, though. Instead, he went to the side of the house, but the smoke was even thicker and they all started to cough. They definitely couldn't stay here much longer or they'd die.

They went to the one room that Nicky hadn't expected them to go—the sunroom. It was literally all glass except for the roof and door frame. And maybe that's why Holden had chosen it. Because their attacker probably wouldn't think they would try to escape this way.

"Once we're outside stay low and move fast," Holden added. "We'll need to get to the barn."

That was all he said before they started running. Holden unlocked the door, threw it open and they hurried out into the night. It was terrifying to be out in the open, but at least the smoke wasn't as bad here so she could breathe.

Nicky tried to keep her gun ready as they ran toward the barn. If this had been normal circumstances, it wouldn't have been that far—only about twenty yards—but it felt as if it was miles.

Other than some shrubs and a few scattered trees, there wasn't much they could use for cover, but when they reached one of the large oaks, Holden pulled them behind it and glanced around. Probably trying to make sure someone wasn't already waiting for them at the barn.

Nicky cursed because she couldn't see much of anything, but it tapped into one of her phobias. Mercy, she hated the darkness and, in this case, everything that it could conceal. She prayed their attackers hadn't had time yet to make it to this part of the grounds.

"Let's go," Holden said.

They started running again, but instead of making a beeline toward the barn, Holden continued to use the trees for cover. They darted behind another oak. Then another. Until the barn was only about ten yards away.

Now that they were closer, Nicky tried to pick through the darkness to see if Minton or the attackers were there. She didn't see anything, but Holden must have thought their chances were better in the barn than behind the tree because he motioned for them to get moving again. They did. But they'd barely made it a step.

When someone fired a shot at them.

FROM THE MOMENT he'd seen the SUV pull up in front of the house, Holden had figured it would come down to this.

To an attack.

Later he would curse himself for not being able to prevent it. But for now, he had to protect Nicky before these goons could kill her.

Holden pulled her to the ground and hoped that he hadn't hurt her arm in the process. It wasn't a serious injury, but just bumping it could cause a lot of pain. Enough that she wouldn't be able to think straight, and right now he needed all three of them thinking straight.

Shooting straight as well.

"Keep watch that way," Holden told Kara when she landed on the ground next to them. He tipped his head toward the barn. He didn't want anyone sneaking up on them from behind and ambushing them.

"Nicky, you keep an eye on the right side of the house," Holden added. "But stay down."

She gave a shaky nod. Actually, she was shaking all over, but that didn't stop her from lifting her gun and aiming it at the right side of the house.

There was another shot.

It smacked into the tree in the spot where Holden had just been standing. Whoever had fired was obviously in good position to see them.

But where?

He cursed the darkness and looked around but couldn't pinpoint the location of the shooter.

Holden's phone dinged, and because he didn't want to lose focus, he took it from his pocket and handed it to Nicky.

"It's from Grayson," she said when she read the text message. "He's still about fifteen minutes out."

Fifteen minutes was an eternity when they were under attack like this. "Text him back and tell him about the gunfire. And the fire in Kayla's house. I want him to approach with sirens blaring."

That might not do much to deter their attackers, but at least the thugs would know that backup had arrived and that maybe they were outgunned.

Holden still didn't have a clue how many they were up against.

There could be an entire army of hired guns out there now. With the commotion of the grenade blasts, the fire and their escape, a dozen more vehicles could have pulled in front of the house by now.

There was another shot, and this time Holden got a glimpse of the shooter. He was at the left rear side of the house, but the moment he fired, he ducked back behind cover. Holden took aim, waiting for the idiot to lean out again so that he'd have a decent shot.

"I just saw someone near the barn," Kara whispered.

"Minton?"

"Hard to tell, but I think the person might have gone inside. Either that, or he's on the ground just outside the barn."

Not good. Because Holden didn't have many options here, and the barn was the nearest building.

The tree wasn't big enough to give them good cover, especially if someone launched another grenade at them. Of course, they could fire a grenade into there, too, but to do that, they'd have to come out into the open.

Like the shooter on the left of the house.

He finally leaned out again, and Holden didn't waste a second. He took aim and fired. Two shots. They slammed into the guy's chest, and he went down. Probably not dead, though. He was almost certainly wearing body armor, but the shots were enough to knock him off his feet.

"Let's move," Holden told them.

They hurried from the cover of the tree, staying as low as they could. With each step Holden prayed that there wouldn't be any more shots fired at him, but he knew it was only a matter of time before the gunman's partners realized he was down, and they would no doubt pick up where he left off.

Holden didn't see Minton or anyone else near the barn. It didn't mean someone wasn't there, though. That's why he darted inside just ahead of Nicky and Kara. He and Kara both brought up their guns, their gazes slashing from one side of the barn to the other.

"Stay close to me," Holden whispered to Nicky.

It was dark inside, too dark to see much of anything, and Holden didn't like that the back doors were wide-open as well. That had probably been intentional since there was nothing stored in the barn, but with both doors open, their attackers could trap them.

"Keep watch out back," Holden told Kara, and he moved to the side of the front door so he could look for more gunmen.

Nothing.

Well, nothing except for the fact that Kayla's house was now in flames. Kayla had done them a huge favor by letting them stay there, and now her house would be destroyed. Even if the fire department made it there in time, they wouldn't be able to get onto the grounds until it was secure.

It was far from being secure, and Holden got proof of that when he saw another gunman. This guy was on the opposite side of the house from his fallen comrade. He didn't lean out but rather fired, still using the house for cover.

But he didn't fire into the barn.

The shot went to the pasture area just on the side of it.

It didn't stay just a single shot, either. The guy fired another one. Then another. However, even over the thick gunfire, Holden heard something else he certainly hadn't expected to hear.

"Help me!" someone called out.

Beatrice.

What the hell was she doing here?

"Help me!" Beatrice screamed again, and

with that scream still echoing in Holden's head, he heard the movement at the back of the barn. And a moment later, Beatrice came running.

Chapter Seventeen

Nicky pivoted, taking aim at Beatrice. Kara did as well. But Holden stayed put, volleying glances over his shoulder while he kept watch at the front.

"Put up your hands," Kara immediately ordered the woman.

Beatrice stopped in her tracks when she saw the two guns pointed at her, and she shook her head. "Someone's trying to kill me," Beatrice insisted.

"Yeah, and it'll be me who does that if you don't put up your hands," Holden assured her.

"I'm the victim here," Beatrice said through a heavy sob. "Someone kidnapped me and forced me to come to—" she glanced around "—wherever this place is."

Nicky wasn't ready to believe that just yet. Maybe not ever. Because after all, Beatrice was one of their suspects, and she could have come running in there to ambush them.

Except Beatrice wasn't armed.

And her hands were tied behind her back.

Other than the plastic cuffs around her wrists, she was wearing one of her usual blue skirts and tops. Heels, too, even though one of them was broken. Her hair was a tangled mess, and there was either a bruise or some dirt on her face.

Beatrice certainly looked as if she might have been kidnapped, but Nicky still wasn't buying it. She could have had someone put those plastic cuffs on her to make it seem as if she'd been kidnapped. And the only reason she would have had for doing that was to get close enough to kill them.

Apparently Kara wasn't buying it, either. She went to the woman and frisked her. "Sit there," Kara ordered.

The deputy used the barrel of her gun to motion toward one of the handful of bales of hay that was in the barn. It was the nearest one to the door.

Outside, some more shots came, and these slammed into the barn. Holden had to move to the side and he motioned for Nicky and Kara to do the same.

"Quit treating me like a criminal," Beatrice

snarled despite the deafening gunfire. "I didn't have anything to do with this."

"Yeah, right," Holden mumbled. "Don't let her out of your sight," he added to Nicky and Kara.

Nicky had no intention of doing that, but she also kept watch at the back doors. She wanted to shut them, but that would put her in the possible line of fire if there were indeed kidnappers or gunmen out there.

More shots came, and Holden leaned out just long enough to fire some shots of his own. Maybe that would keep the gunmen at bay until Grayson and the others could arrive.

"Who *kidnapped* you?" Nicky asked Beatrice, and she didn't bother to sound as if she believed the woman.

It took Beatrice a moment to finish the sob she was in the middle of so she could answer. "Some men wearing ski masks. They looked like the same ones who had the baby."

Oh, God. The baby. That tightened Nicky's chest. "Is your son here, too?"

Beatrice shook her head, kept on crying. "No. He was at the house with the nanny and his bodyguards. I was on my way to Lee's office when the men ran me off the road and took me at gunpoint."

"What do they want with you?" Holden

snapped. "And why would they just let you go so you could come running into the barn where we just happen to be?"

Holden had Nicky beat in the skepticism department.

"They didn't *let* me go," Beatrice insisted. "I escaped. I was in the SUV when they started shooting those grenade things at the house. When two of them got out, I managed to get the door opened. I got out and started running. I ended up here. Didn't you see that man shooting at me?"

Beatrice looked at Holden when she asked that question, and Nicky glanced at him, too. He nodded. A surprise. Nicky had heard the shots, but she'd thought the gunman was shooting at Holden.

"The man could have been shooting into the ground or over your head," Holden added. "That doesn't prove you're innocent."

No, but it did lead Nicky to her next question. "How many men brought you here?"

"Three," Beatrice answered without hesitation.

If the woman was telling the truth, then that meant there were only two of them left since Holden had shot one of them. But maybe that wounded one was still capable of doing some damage.

There were more shots, but Nicky also heard something else. A welcome sound this time.

Sirens.

Grayson was close now, and it wouldn't be long before he was on the grounds. Nicky had no idea how close he could get to the house, but she hoped he and the deputies would be able to put a stop to this.

A permanent stop.

That meant capturing at least one of the gunmen alive so he could tell them who'd hired him. Nicky had to believe that could happen because there was no way Holden, she and the twins could continue to live like this.

"Get down!" Holden called out to them. He charged toward Nicky, pulling her to the ground just as the explosion tore through the barn.

Holden and she both fell, and even though she knew it wasn't intentional, his arm hit hers, and the pain shot through her. Nicky had to fight for breath, and her eyes watered.

But that was the least of their problems.

Their attackers had obviously launched another grenade their way, and it had taken off a good portion of the front of the barn. They didn't just have the open doors to worry about, there was a hole large enough to drive an SUV through. And maybe that's what they had in mind because Nicky also heard the sound of an engine.

Beatrice was screaming now, perhaps because the impact had sent her to the floor, too, but Nicky couldn't tell if it was Beatrice or Kara who was hurt. However, Kara was at least able to move because she hurried to Beatrice and dragged her away from some of the barn roof that was creaking and ready to fall.

Holden pulled Nicky to her feet as well, and he ran to the back of the barn with her. "Watch behind us," he told her.

Nicky did that as best she could, and she saw the source of that engine. It was the SUV all right, and it was coming right toward them.

Holden pushed her behind him and fired. His bullets went right into the windshield. Kara shot at the tires, and the SUV finally came to a stop in the yard. Still, it was close. Too close. And those gunmen could start shooting or launch another grenade at them.

"We have to move," Holden said, and he turned, no doubt to get them started out the back door.

But it was too late.

The man came rushing in, and he was armed. It happened so fast, and while Holden was trying to get into position to fire, the man latched onto Beatrice. That's when Nicky got a better look at his face.

It was Lee Minton.

And he put a gun to his wife's head.

HOLDEN DEFINITELY DIDN'T need this. Whatever the *hell* this was.

"What are you doing?" Holden demanded.

"I'm getting her to confess," Minton said, his voice as shaky as his hand. Not a good combination to have a gun in the hands of a man who was clearly out of control. "She's the one who had me kidnapped." He jammed the gun even harder against Beatrice's head. "Admit it."

Beatrice didn't deny it, and she started sobbing again.

"Now isn't the time for this," Holden assured him. He kept watch on that SUV. On Minton, too.

But if Minton heard him, he didn't acknowledge it. The man had clearly worked himself up into a rage.

"I want to hear her admit it," Minton growled. "And don't lie, Beatrice, because I have the proof. The thug you hired confessed. You knew that, and that's why you had me kidnapped again."

"No!" Beatrice practically shouted. She winced when he dug the gun into her skin. "Yes, I did have you taken the first time. But not now. I had no part in this, I swear." She looked up at Holden and repeated that.

Maybe she was telling the truth, but Holden didn't care. She'd just admitted to kidnapping her husband, and it didn't matter if she'd done that once or twice. It meant she was capable of pretty much anything.

"There are two men with a grenade launcher in that SUV, and he can take down the rest of this barn with just one more blast," Holden reminded the senator.

Again, Minton didn't seem to hear Holden. "How could you have done that to me?" he shouted to his wife. "I always knew you were a gold digger, but I never expected you to have me kidnapped. And why? So you could get your hands on my money."

Holden was ready to throttle them both. "You can stay here and die," he finally told Minton. "Or you can try to get out of here with us."

Though Holden did have a problem with Beatrice tagging along. Since she was still wearing the plastic cuffs, she wasn't an immediate danger to them, but she could always call out to the thugs.

Holden looked out at the pasture just as his phone buzzed, and he saw the message from Grayson on the screen.

We're coming in. Watch your fire.

That was a reminder for Holden not to shoot unless he was certain of his target.

Behind them, the SUV started to move, and Holden knew he had to get moving as well. "Come on," Holden told Nicky, and he led them out the door.

He didn't get far, though.

Because the moment he stepped outside, someone put a gun in his face. And it wasn't one of the hired thugs.

It was Amanda.

"Move one inch," she warned him, "and I'll kill you."

Hell. How could he have let this happen? With the noise from the sirens and Minton's and Beatrice's chatter, he hadn't heard the woman approach. That could be the thing that got Nicky and the rest of them killed.

Amanda backed him into the barn and put the gun to his head. Holden still had his weapon. So did the others. But if he moved or did anything sudden, Amanda could shoot. And not necessarily shoot him, either. She could turn the gun on Nicky or Kara.

"I was beginning to wonder if you'd ever come out of there," Amanda complained. "I didn't want my men to have to fire off another grenade. Boys, you can come out now," she added, and it took Holden a moment to realize she was speaking into a small communicator clipped to her collar.

The *boys* were two armed thugs who got out of the SUV. And they weren't wearing ski masks. Definitely not good. Because it meant Amanda and the two guys intended to kill all of them.

"You want me to move the SUV to the back?" one of the thugs asked Amanda.

"No. I can't be sure the lawmen haven't made it back there."

That was a possibility, too, since Grayson would know the layout of the grounds. Plus, Grayson could have sent some deputies to one of the ranch trails that threaded all around the property.

"Guns on the ground *now*," the thug snarled, glancing at Holden, Nicky and Kara. He stayed near the front, and the other hurried to Amanda's side.

Without so much as a warning, the guy at the front took aim at Kara and fired, the shot slamming into her arm.

Damn. It took everything inside Holden to stop himself from charging the guy. But if he did, it would just get Kara killed. Kara groaned in pain and dropped to her knees.

"Weapons down now," the thug repeated. "Or the next shot goes right into her head."

They had no choice but to drop their weapons. Minton, however, kept his gun hidden on the side of his leg. Maybe Amanda and her goons hadn't seen it.

"This is how this will work," Amanda said, her voice so cold that he felt the chill all the way to his bones. "Beatrice and the senator will come with me. If they don't cooperate, I'll start putting bullets into them until they do."

"Because you need to set them up to take the blame for all of this," Holden said. It was just a theory, but he could tell from Amanda's slight smile that he was right.

Amanda was going to take Minton and Beatrice to a secondary location, where she could either force them to make a false confession or else plant something incriminating on them. The perfect way to end that would be to have their deaths look like a murder-suicide.

"How do you intend to get out of here?" Nicky snapped. "Backup has arrived."

"Yes." Amanda didn't show any emotion about that. "That's where you and Holden come in. I have some more men in place now, and they should be able to take care of any extra Silver Creek lawmen. But I need hostages, human shields, whatever you want to call it. Either way, we're leaving."

"But you'll have to take Nicky with you, too," Holden said. It was yet another theory. "Because you'll have to make sure she doesn't have copies of those files from Conceptions."

"I'm sure Nicky will tell me all about those to save you from dying a really painful death. Those files have other encrypted data in them," she added. "I will get them back."

Hell, that meant there could be other babies. Or at least plans to continue this sick surrogacy operation.

"You murdered a man," Nicky snapped. "You killed Paul."

Amanda didn't confirm that. Didn't have to. She'd ordered Paul's death when he wouldn't give her the files, and she would do the same to Nicky. Or at least she'd try. Holden only hoped Amanda didn't have one of her goons shoot him before he could put a stop to this.

Amanda motioned toward one of the thugs, and he went closer to Minton, taking aim at the senator. "What part of 'put down your gun' didn't you understand?"

Holden's stomach dropped. So, they'd seen Minton's gun after all.

The thug didn't add more to that order to Minton, probably because Amanda's threat had been enough. If Minton didn't cooperate, Amanda or one of the gunmen would shoot him.

Minton dropped the gun, and the moment it hit the ground, the thug came toward them. He latched onto Beatrice by her hair, yanking her to her feet. Beatrice yelled in pain, but he only whacked her upside the head with his weapon. When she collapsed, the guy threw her over his shoulder and started toward the SUV.

The sound of gunfire cracked through the air.

It was close, somewhere near the front of the house, and Holden prayed that none of the lawmen had been hurt. More shots came though. A flurry of gunfire.

"Wait just a few seconds," Amanda told the guy, and she added a profanity under her breath.

Maybe she'd expected that her lackeys could have finished off Grayson and the others by now. Or at least kept them at bay so they could start the process of getting the heck out of there.

The moments crawled by, and Holden glanced at Kara to see how she was holding up. She was bleeding and needed medical attention fast. That wasn't going to happen, though, until the danger had been neutralized. Since the gunfire was continuing, that might not be for a while.

"Just hang in there," Holden said to Kara.

Nicky looked at him. She didn't say anything, but he could tell she was silently asking him what to do. Holden wasn't sure, not yet anyway. However, he knew if they got in that SUV, they'd be dead as soon as Amanda no longer needed them.

The shots outside finally stopped, and Amanda motioned for her man to get moving. The guy did, taking Minton and Beatrice toward the front of the barn and the SUV.

"Your turn," Amanda said to Nicky. "Go with Beatrice and the senator."

Nicky didn't jump to do that, but Holden nodded. She still hesitated but finally took several steps toward the thug who was in the process of tossing Beatrice into the vehicle.

Amanda put her mouth against Holden's ear. "Of course, you won't be going with them," she whispered. "Can't risk that since you and the deputy here would only try to kill us the first chance you get."

Holden had figured that out. Nicky was the only hostage Amanda needed, and the only reason the woman hadn't already tried to kill him was because she was using him to get Nicky to cooperate.

Nicky probably couldn't hear what the woman was saying, but she stopped, and stared at him.

"Keep moving!" the thug snarled, and after he stuffed the senator in the SUV, he started for Nicky.

Nothing about this was ideal, especially not with the armed goon right next to Amanda, but Holden figured it was now or never. He had to do something. He turned, slamming his body into Amanda's, hoping to knock the gun from her hand.

He didn't.

Amanda pulled the trigger.

EVERYTHING SEEMED TO FREEZE.

Nicky yelled for Holden to get down, but the shot drowned out her voice. The sound was deafening, and it roared through the barn. Roared through her, too, and for some heart-stopping moments, Nicky thought Amanda had managed to shoot Holden.

And maybe she had.

It was hard to tell because Holden rammed into Amanda and her hired gun and sent all three of them crashing to the ground. Amanda screamed. Maybe because she was in pain. After all, she'd had a C-section just the week before. But judging from the profanity that followed, Amanda was also enraged at what Holden had done.

Kara scrambled across the floor toward the gun, causing the thug to take aim at her. Nicky couldn't just stand there and let him shoot the deputy again so she charged toward him. As Holden had done to Amanda, she plowed into him. She didn't hit him with her injured arm, but the jolt from the impact was painful enough. It was like ramming into a brick wall.

Unlike Amanda and the hired gun who'd been next to her, the brute didn't fall. However, he did stagger back just a little, and Nicky ducked out of the way to stop him from shooting or punching her. It was only a handful of seconds. But it was enough time for Kara to get the gun. She fired two shots at him.

That brought him down.

He dropped, clutching his chest, and that's when Nicky realized that Kara's shots had gone into the guy's Kevlar vest. He wasn't dead. He'd just had the breath knocked out of him. That meant she only had a couple of minutes to help Holden while the guy was out of commission.

Outside, there was the sound of more gunfire, closer than it had been before, and maybe that meant Grayson and the deputies were coming to help.

"Watch him," Nicky told Kara, and she hoped the wounded deputy could shoot again if it came down to it. Kara was shaking, but she still managed to keep her gun aimed at the guy.

Nicky scooped up her gun and ran to Holden, but she still couldn't tell if he was injured. There was blood, but in the darkness it was impossible to see who was bleeding.

Impossible for Nicky to have a clean shot, either.

The thug was punching Holden, hard, and

while Holden was fighting back, Amanda had latched onto his arm to prevent him from delivering a blow that would have stopped the gunman.

Amanda was also moaning in pain, and her moans turned to a shriek when her own man accidentally elbowed her. She rolled to the side, clutching her stomach, but she didn't move far enough away from Holden so that Nicky could shoot her. Worse, Amanda still had her gun.

A gun she pointed at Nicky.

Nicky jumped to the side just as Amanda pulled the trigger, and the bullet slammed into the SUV. Amanda howled out a feral sound, a mix of rage and pain, and she scrambled away from the fight. Before Nicky could take aim at her, Amanda limped out the back of the barn.

"No!" Nicky yelled. She couldn't get away.

But Nicky couldn't risk Holden being killed, either. She didn't run after the woman, and she still didn't have a clean shot so she kicked the thug in the head as hard as she could. The thug reached for her, trying to grab onto her leg.

Holden didn't let that happen, though.

"Move back," Holden shouted to her, and he snatched the guy's gun.

The thug didn't give up his weapon, though. He rammed his elbow into Holden's jaw. Holden's head flopped back, and Nicky saw something she didn't want to see. More blood.

And the man put his meaty grip around Holden's hand and gun.

The fight was on again. But it didn't last long. Because there was the sickening sound of a shot being fired. Nicky could have sworn her heart skipped some beats, and it took her several terrifying moments to realize who'd been shot.

Not Holden, thank God.

It was the hired gun.

Holden didn't waste any time pushing the guy off him. In the same motion, he got to his feet and started out the back of the barn.

Going after Amanda, no doubt.

However, Nicky didn't know if Amanda was out there alone or if there were other gunmen. There was still some shooting going on toward the front of the house, but it was possible one or more hired thugs had come near the barn to make sure their boss got out of this alive.

Even though Nicky knew Holden wouldn't approve, she followed him, watching to make sure he wasn't about to be ambushed. She didn't see any hired guns, nor did she see Amanda at first. That's because the woman was on the side of the barn, probably trying to get to the SUV.

Amanda hadn't made it far, mainly because she was staggering and practically doubled over.

Nicky had no idea how long it took for a C-section incision to heal, but she suspected a week hadn't been nearly enough time. The pain didn't stop Amanda from turning and aiming her gun at Holden.

She fired.

Holden ducked behind the back of the barn, stepping in front of Nicky. "Watch behind us," he said.

Nicky did while Holden took aim at Amanda. There was no place for the woman to run for cover, and the SUV was still several yards away from her.

"Put down your gun," Holden ordered Amanda.

She laughed, but there was definitely no humor in it. "If you kill me, you'll never know if there are other babies from the Genesis Project."

Nicky's stomach twisted and turned at hearing that. Mercy, if there were more, they needed to find them.

"Put down your gun," Holden repeated.

Amanda didn't answer. Not with words anyway. She fired another shot, this one slamming into the barn. Holden cursed, leaned out and fired.

Even though Nicky couldn't actually see the woman, she knew Amanda had been hit. No mistaking the sound of the bullet hitting human flesh.

Holden tossed Nicky his phone, and he hurried toward Amanda. "Call Grayson and tell him to get an ambulance out here *fast*."

Chapter Eighteen

Holden paced across the break room of the sheriff's office because he didn't know how else to burn off some of this restless energy inside him. He felt ready to explode, but he had to keep it together. Not only for Nicky's sake, but also because they'd be seeing the twins soon, and he didn't want them picking up on the stress.

Nicky seemed past the point of having any restless energy. Or any energy at all for that matter. She was lying on the small sofa, staring up at the ceiling. Added to that, he could count on one hand how many sentences she'd said to him in the hour since they'd left Kayla's place.

She might be in shock, was almost certainly dealing with the adrenaline crash, but she'd still been vocal enough to insist on not going to the hospital to be checked.

Holden hadn't liked that, but at least she

didn't have any visible injuries. Unlike Kara and Amanda. They had both been taken by ambulance to the hospital and were in surgery.

"It shouldn't be long now before we can leave," Holden said to Nicky.

She looked at him and nodded, and while she wasn't exactly jumping up and down, he figured she wanted to see the babies as much as he did. Especially now that it was safe to do that.

Amanda's thugs had been rounded up. At least the ones who were still alive. Grayson and the other deputies who'd responded to the scene had been forced to kill three men. Added to the one that Holden had shot in the barn, that left two, and last he'd heard, they were in holding cells awaiting interrogation.

Something that Holden wouldn't be doing.

He wanted answers—too much—and with all the emotions bubbling up inside of him, he might beat them senseless if they didn't tell him what he wanted to know. Besides, he didn't want to leave Nicky.

Holden went closer to the sofa, and Nicky scooted over so he could sit next to her. "If Amanda dies," she said, "how will we find out if there are other babies?"

He'd already thought about that a lot. "The

files you took. Amanda said there was encrypted information in them."

"She could have been lying," Nicky pointed out.

He shook his head. "It was important for her to get those files." Heck, she'd been willing to kill to get them. So there had to be something she wanted concealed in them. "The FBI's going over them now, and they'll find whatever it is."

He hoped.

Nicky went back into silent mode for a moment, but then she reached out and touched the front of his shirt. "You should probably change that before we see the twins."

Holden glanced down and cursed when he saw the blood. It wasn't his blood or even Nicky's, thank God. It belonged to the thug he'd shot in the barn, but he definitely didn't want to hold his niece and nephew while wearing a bloody shirt.

There was a row of lockers on the wall, and Holden rummaged through them until he found one of Gage's shirts. Since they were about the same size, Holden knew it would fit and he stripped off his dirty clothes.

And Nicky gasped.

She got off the sofa as if something had

scalded her, and she hurried to him. "You're hurt. You said you were all right."

By all right, he meant alive and not seriously injured. But yes, there were bruises, cuts and scrapes over most of his torso. His hands, too. It came with the territory of getting into a fist-fight with a jerk who'd outsized him.

"Minor stuff," he assured her.

But Nicky didn't take his word for it. She ran her fingertips over one of the bruises. Which meant she ran those fingertips over his bare stomach. Holden would had to have been dead not to react to her touch. He reacted even more when she turned him around and explored the injuries to his back.

"This feels a little like foreplay," he joked.

She stepped around to face him, but that certainly wasn't a joking look in her eyes. It was tears. "You could have been killed," she said on a rise of breath.

Yeah, a couple of times over. It was the same for her, but Holden didn't want to remind either of them of that. Instead, he pulled her into his arms, and even though this was a hug of comfort, it felt like foreplay, too, since he was shirtless.

"It'll all be okay," he said, and he brushed a kiss on her forehead.

Holden also tried not to put pressure on any

of her injuries. In addition to the stitches on her arm, he could see some bruises on her now. That certainly didn't help with all this extra energy inside him and was verification that he needed to stay far away from those captured gunmen. He wanted someone to pay for every injury on Nicky's body.

"Will it really be okay?" she asked, looking up at him.

"Yes." And Holden kissed her to prove it.

Of course, the kiss didn't prove anything except that he was attracted to her and that he cared for her, but maybe that would ease some of her worries. It didn't, though. When she pulled back from the kiss, the worry was still there.

So Holden kissed her again.

This time he deepened it, and he lingered a bit, easing her closer and closer until her body was right against his. Finally, he got a different look from her. Not nearly as much worry, and there was some heat mixed with it. But it wasn't nearly enough heat as far as Holden was concerned so he went back for a third kiss. He would have given a fourth, too, if he hadn't heard the footsteps.

"Interrupting anything?" Gage asked.

His cousin was already in the doorway of the break room before Nicky and Holden moved away from each other. It was too late, though, because Gage had already seen them. And it was a reminder to Holden that his family should see Nicky and him like this. He slipped his arm back around her, only to get another reminder.

That he was still shirtless.

Gage smiled again. "Why don't you go ahead and get dressed? It's time for us to leave for the safe house."

"Grayson gave the okay for that?" Holden quickly put on the shirt, trying not to wince when the movement caused his banged-up body to ache.

"He did. I can give you an update along the way."

Holden hoped those updates included lots and lots of good news because he wasn't sure Nicky could handle anything else tonight. Heck, Holden didn't want to handle any more bad news, either. He and Nicky had enough nightmares to last them a couple of lifetimes.

They made their way to the squad room, and Holden saw something that caused him to stop moving. Minton, and he was holding his son. Holden recognized the look on the senator's face. Love. Minton was already smitten with the newborn.

"Minton wanted his son here while he was giving his statement," Gage explained.

At the sound of his name, Minton turned and looked at Nicky and Holden. "Thank you," he said. "For everything."

Holden had been concerned as to the fate of the Minton baby, but he wasn't as concerned now. It was obvious the kid was in loving hands.

"What about Beatrice?" Nicky asked.

Minton's mouth tightened. "She's at the county jail where I hope she'll stay."

"She will," Gage assured him, and he turned to Holden and Nicky to finish his explanation. "The kidnapper Beatrice hired is testifying against her in exchange for a lesser sentence. Beatrice is being charged with kidnapping, forced imprisonment and some other charges."

"But Beatrice didn't have anything to do with the Genesis Project?" Holden added.

"No. There's no evidence she did anyway. That was all Amanda's doing."

Too bad. Because if Beatrice had been a co-conspirator, then she could have been offered her own deal if she helped them find out if there were any other babies.

Holden wished the senator good luck, and he and Nicky were about to leave when someone stepped out from one of the interview rooms.

Oscar.

Nicky groaned, which expressed Holden's sentiment. "I don't have time for another round of your threats," Nicky snapped. "You're not taking custody of Annie and Emmett's babies."

The muscles stirred in Oscar's jaw. "No. I'm not."

Nicky's shoulders came back. "Is this some kind of trick?"

"No. The sheriff is charging me with obstruction of justice for not reporting that I was with the kidnappers when they got the ransom from Beatrice. I don't think a judge will grant me custody after that. Do you?"

Holden hoped not.

Oscar didn't seem as bitter about that as Holden thought he would be. He looked defeated. "I'd like the see the babies," Oscar added.

Nicky glanced at Holden to see what his take was on this, but Holden didn't have one at the moment. "You're their grandfather," Holden finally said. "My advice is when you start acting like one—a good, decent one—then you'll get to see them."

Oscar didn't argue with that. He simply turned and went back into the interview room. Soon, Holden and Nicky would need to sit down with him and work out some ground rules for any future contact with the twins. For now, though, Holden just wanted to get out of there.

Nicky clearly felt the same, so they followed Gage to a cruiser. Even though they were certain they'd rounded up all of Amanda's thugs, they still hurried.

It might take a while before either one of them could step outside and not relive the memories of the attacks.

Holden got into the backseat with Nicky, and Gage took the wheel. It shouldn't take long for them to get to the safe house. Which was good. It was already late, and he didn't want to be in crash-and-burn mode when they got there. Not just because of the babies, either. Because he wanted to talk some things over with Nicky.

The problem was—Holden didn't know which things.

"First the good news," Gage said once he'd pulled away from the station. "Kara's going to be fine. The doc got her all stitched up, and she's already asking when she can come back to work."

That was a relief. The only reason Kara had been in that barn was because she'd been trying to help Nicky and him, and it would have been a hard blow if she'd lost her life because of it.

Still, as good as the news was, Holden couldn't celebrate because he figured if there was good news, then Gage was about to deliver some bad.

And he did.

"Amanda died in surgery," Gage said.

That felt like a punch right in the gut. Not only because Amanda couldn't tell them about those files, but also because Holden had been the one to kill her. Of course, she hadn't given him any choice but to shoot her. Still, it ate away at him to think he'd taken a life.

"Did Amanda happen to say anything before she died?" Nicky asked.

"No. She never regained consciousness after she was shot."

It wasn't much consolation, but Amanda probably wouldn't have said anything even if she had been awake. Not without a sweet plea deal on the table, and since she'd had a man murdered, that wouldn't have happened.

"So, what about you two?" Gage asked. "And yeah, I'm talking about that kissing you were doing in the break room."

"What about it?" Holden countered, mainly because he didn't know how to answer Gage's question.

What about Nicky and him?

And Holden looked at Nicky to see if she had the answer.

She didn't, not a verbal one anyway, but all in all it was a darn good way to respond. She kissed him. It wasn't one of those scorchers they'd shared in the break room, but it went a long way to soothing some of that acid inside him. In fact, it made him smile.

It was short-lived though because Holden's phone buzzed, and he saw Grayson's name on the screen. Holden put it on speaker so that Nicky and Gage could hear, but he hoped it wasn't another round of bad news.

"Did Gage tell you that Amanda died?" Grayson asked the moment Holden answered.

"Yeah. And that Kara was okay."

"She is. Something else is okay, too. One of Amanda's gunmen is cooperating. He's going to give the FBI info about the encryption."

"Thank God," Nicky said, her voice barely a whisper, and she repeated it several times.

"Are there other babies?" Holden asked.

"He says yes. There's one more. Not Emmett and Annie's baby, though," Grayson quickly added. "A surrogate is carrying a baby who belongs to a wealthy lawyer and his wife. The FBI will contact both the couple and the surrogate."

Good. It wasn't the ideal way for a couple to find out they were about to be parents, but since they'd gone to Conceptions Clinic that meant they'd been serious about having a child. And now they would get one. Holden made a mental note to check on them when things settled down a bit.

Whenever that would be.

"I'll keep you posted if we learn anything else from the files," Grayson went on. "But the gunman is convinced that's the last baby out there."

Four babies in total. And Amanda had two million of the four she'd planned to get. Heck, this could have just been phase one of her operation, too. All she had to do was find other embryos of wealthy parents and do the same thing to them that she'd done to the Mintons, the other couple and the Rylands.

"Where will you be taking the twins when you leave the safe house?" Grayson asked.

Good question, and Holden had to think about it for a couple of seconds. "For now, we'll go to my place near Silver Creek Ranch." His house wasn't on the main part of the ranch but rather on the land adjacent. He looked at Nicky to see if she was okay with that.

She nodded. "I wasn't exactly looking forward to going back to my house since the last time I was there, we were attacked."

Yeah, Holden remembered, and he was glad she'd agreed to go to the ranch. Except she hadn't, not really. That nod could have simply been to give her approval for the twins to go there.

"I'll call you if there are any updates," Grayson added, and he ended the call.

Holden put away his phone, but he wasn't

finished with this conversation. "You're going to Silver Creek Ranch with me," Holden told Nicky.

Then he frowned.

That came out like an order, and judging from Nicky's expression she didn't approve of that any more than he did.

Gage chuckled. "Uh, you do know how to talk to a woman, don't you, cuz?"

Holden frowned even more, and he shut the Plexiglas slider between the seats, but it was hard to be angry with Gage since he was right. Apparently, Holden had lost the ability to speak to a woman.

Well, the only woman that mattered right now anyway.

"Kissing usually works," Nicky said, and the corner of her mouth came up a little.

She was right. So that's what Holden did. He kissed her again. It not only soothed his nerves, but it also reminded him of why this was easy. Easy because he knew now what he needed to say to her.

"I want you to come to my house," he amended. "Maybe not tonight because it's late, but first thing in the morning."

Nicky nodded.

It was the exact response Holden wanted so he kissed her again. The taste of her slid right through him, another reminder that he wanted a whole lot more from her. And not just kisses and sex, either. Now if he could only get the right words to come out of his mouth.

"I'll say it if you will," Nicky whispered.

Holden looked at her, to make sure they were on the same page. They were, but he kissed her to confirm it.

"I love you," Nicky said at the exact moment, Holden said, "I love you."

Yep, same page all right.

"Took you long enough to figure it out," Gage joked. Then he laughed.

Holden tuned him out because he wasn't done yet. Might never be done when it came to Nicky.

"I want it all," Holden said to her. "Raising the twins—together. Marriage. I'll even build a white picket fence. Just think about it and give me your answer."

Holden was willing to wait. However long it took, but Nicky didn't have to think on it for long. "Yes, to raising the twins together. Yes, to the marriage. The fence is optional."

Smiling, she caught onto the front of Holden's shirt and pulled him to her, and Nicky kissed him.

* * * * *

Look for USA TODAY *bestselling author
Delores Fossen's next book in*
THE LAWMEN OF SILVER
CREEK RANCH *miniseries,* DRURY,
when it goes on sale next month.

*You'll find it wherever
Harlequin Intrigue books are sold!*

LARGER-PRINT BOOKS!

HARLEQUIN *Presents*®

GET 2 FREE LARGER-PRINT NOVELS PLUS 2 FREE GIFTS!

PASSION GUARANTEED SEDUCTION

YES! Please send me 2 FREE LARGER-PRINT Harlequin Presents® novels and my 2 FREE gifts (gifts are worth about $10). After receiving them, if I don't wish to receive any more books, I can return the shipping statement marked "cancel." If I don't cancel, I will receive 6 brand-new novels every month and be billed just $5.30 per book in the U.S. or $5.74 per book in Canada. That's a saving of at least 12% off the cover price! It's quite a bargain! Shipping and handling is just 50¢ per book in the U.S. and 75¢ per book in Canada.* I understand that accepting the 2 free books and gifts places me under no obligation to buy anything. I can always return a shipment and cancel at any time. Even if I never buy another book, the two free books and gifts are mine to keep forever.

176/376 HDN GHVY

Name	(PLEASE PRINT)

Address	Apt. #

City	State/Prov.	Zip/Postal Code

Signature (if under 18, a parent or guardian must sign)

Mail to the **Reader Service:**
IN U.S.A.: P.O. Box 1867, Buffalo, NY 14240-1867
IN CANADA: P.O. Box 609, Fort Erie, Ontario L2A 5X3

**Are you a subscriber to Harlequin Presents® books
and want to receive the larger-print edition?
Call 1-800-873-8635 today or visit us at www.ReaderService.com.**

* Terms and prices subject to change without notice. Prices do not include applicable taxes. Sales tax applicable in N.Y. Canadian residents will be charged applicable taxes. Offer not valid in Quebec. This offer is limited to one order per household. Not valid for current subscribers to Harlequin Presents Larger-Print books. All orders subject to credit approval. Credit or debit balances in a customer's account(s) may be offset by any other outstanding balance owed by or to the customer. Please allow 4 to 6 weeks for delivery. Offer available while quantities last.

Your Privacy—The Reader Service is committed to protecting your privacy. Our Privacy Policy is available online at www.ReaderService.com or upon request from the Reader Service.

We make a portion of our mailing list available to reputable third parties that offer products we believe may interest you. If you prefer that we not exchange your name with third parties, or if you wish to clarify or modify your communication preferences, please visit us at www.ReaderService.com/consumerschoice or write to us at Reader Service Preference Service, P.O. Box 9062, Buffalo, NY 14240-9062. Include your complete name and address.

HPLP15

LARGER-PRINT BOOKS!

GET 2 FREE LARGER-PRINT NOVELS PLUS
2 FREE GIFTS!

⟨H⟩ HARLEQUIN®

Romance

From the Heart, For the Heart

LARGER-PRINT BOOKS!
GET 2 FREE LARGER-PRINT NOVELS PLUS
2 FREE GIFTS!

H™ HARLEQUIN®

super romance®

More Story...More Romance

WESTERN WP PROMISES

YES! Please send me **The Western Promises Collection** in Larger Print. This collection begins with 3 FREE books and 2 FREE gifts (gifts valued at approx. $14.00 retail) in the first shipment, along with the other first 4 books from the collection! If I do not cancel, I will receive 8 monthly shipments until I have the entire 51-book Western Promises collection. I will receive 2 or 3 FREE books in each shipment and I will pay just $4.99 US/ $5.89 CDN for each of the other four books in each shipment, plus $2.99 for shipping and handling per shipment. *If I decide to keep the entire collection, I'll have paid for only 32 books, because 19 books are FREE! I understand that accepting the 3 free books and gifts places me under no obligation to buy anything. I can always return a shipment and cancel at any time. My free books and gifts are mine to keep no matter what I decide.

272 HCN 3070 472 HCN 3070

Name	(PLEASE PRINT)	
Address		Apt. #
City	State/Prov.	Zip/Postal Code

Signature (if under 18, a parent or guardian must sign)

Mail to the **Reader Service:**
IN U.S.A.: P.O. Box 1867, Buffalo, NY 14240-1867
IN CANADA: P.O. Box 609, Fort Erie, Ontario L2A 5X3